BOOK**SHOTS**

AVAILABLE NOW!

CROSS KILL

Along Came a Spider killer Gary Soneji died years ago. But Alex Cross swears he sees Soneji gun down his partner. Is his greatest enemy back from the grave?

ZOO 2

Humans are evolving into a savage new species that could save civilization—or end it. James Patterson's *Zoo* was just the beginning.

THE TRIAL

An accused killer will do anything to disrupt his own trial, including a courtroom shocker that Lindsay Boxer and the Women's Murder Club will never see coming.

LITTLE BLACK DRESS

Can a little black dress change everything? What begins as one woman's fantasy is about to go too far.

LET'S PLAY MAKE-BELIEVE

Christy and Marty just met, and it's love at first sight. Or is it? One of them is playing a dangerous game—and only one will survive.

CHASE

A man falls to his death in an apparent accident....But why does he have the fingerprints of another man who is already dead? Detective Michael Bennett is on the case.

HUNTED

Someone is luring men from the streets to play a mysterious, high-stakes game. Former Special Forces officer David Shelley goes undercover to shut it down—but will he win?

113 MINUTES

Molly Rourke's son has been murdered. Now she'll do whatever it takes to get justice. No one should underestimate a mother's love....

LEARNING TO RIDE

City girl Madeline Harper never wanted to love a cowboy. But rodeo king Tanner Callen might change her mind...and win her heart.

THE McCULLAGH INN IN MAINE

Chelsea O'Kane escapes to Maine to build a new life—until she runs into Jeremy Holland, an old flame....

SACKING THE QUARTERBACK

Attorney Melissa St. James wins every case. Now, when she's up against football superstar Grayson Knight, her heart is on the line, too.

THE MATING SEASON

Documentary ornithologist Sophie Castle is convinced that her heart belongs only to the birds—until she meets her gorgeous cameraman, Rigg Greensman.

UPCOMING THRILLERS
BOOK**SHOTS**

$10,000,000 MARRIAGE PROPOSAL

A mysterious billboard offering $10 million to get married intrigues three single women in LA. But who is Mr. Right…and is he the perfect match for the lucky winner?

FRENCH KISS

It's hard enough to move to a new city, but now everyone French detective Luc Moncrief cares about is being killed off. Welcome to New York.

KILLER CHEF

Caleb Rooney knows how to do two things: run a food truck and solve a murder. When people suddenly start dying of food-borne illnesses, the stakes are higher than ever.…

THE CHRISTMAS MYSTERY

Two stolen paintings disappear from a Park Avenue murder scene—French detective Luc Moncrief is in for a merry Christmas.

BLACK & BLUE

Detective Harry Blue is determined to take down the serial killer who's abducted several women, but her mission leads to a shocking revelation.

UPCOMING ROMANCES

James Patterson's
BOOKSH⬤TS
Flames

DAZZLING: THE DIAMOND TRILOGY, PART I

To support her artistic career, Siobhan Dempsey works at the elite Stone Room in New York City…never expecting to be swept away by Derick Miller.

RADIANT: THE DIAMOND TRILOGY, PART II

After an explosive breakup with her billionaire boyfriend, Siobhan moves to Detroit to pursue her art. But Derick isn't ready to give her up.

BODYGUARD

Special Agent Abbie Whitmore has only one task: protect Congressman Jonathan Lassiter from a violent cartel's threats. Yet she's never had to do it while falling in love….

HOT WINTER NIGHTS

Allie Thatcher moved to Montana to start fresh as the head of the trauma center. And even though the days are cold, the nights are steamy…especially when she meets search-and-rescue leader Dex Belmont.

"I KNOW WHO KILLED MY SON."

Molly Rourke's son has been murdered…and she knows who's responsible. Now she's taking the law into her own hands.

Never underestimate a mother's love.

Read the shocking new thriller *113 Minutes*, available now from

BOOK**SHOTS**

HUNTED

JAMES PATTERSON
WITH ANDREW HOLMES

BOOK**SHOTS**

BookShots

Little, Brown and Company

New York Boston London

Copyright © 2016 by James Patterson

Hachette Book Group supports the right to free expression and the value of copyright. The purpose of copyright is to encourage writers and artists to produce the creative works that enrich our culture.

The scanning, uploading, and distribution of this book without permission is a theft of the author's intellectual property. If you would like permission to use material from the book (other than for review purposes), please contact permissions@hbgusa.com. Thank you for your support of the author's rights.

BookShots / Little, Brown and Company
Hachette Book Group
1290 Avenue of the Americas, New York, NY 10104
bookshots.com

First Edition: September 2016

BookShots is an imprint of Little, Brown and Company, a division of Hachette Book Group, Inc. The Little, Brown name and logo are trademarks of Hachette Book Group, Inc. The BookShots name and logo are trademarks of JBP Business, LLC.

The publisher is not responsible for websites (or their content) that are not owned by the publisher.

The Hachette Speakers Bureau provides a wide range of authors for speaking events. To find out more, go to hachettespeakersbureau.com or call (866) 376-6591.

ISBN 978-0-316-43088-3
LCCN 2016938307

10 9 8 7 6 5 4 3 2 1

RRD-C

Printed in the United States of America

HUNTED

PART ONE

CHAPTER 1

TWO MEN TROD carefully through the trees in search of their prey. Bluebells and wild garlic were underfoot, beech and Douglas firs on all sides, tendrils of early morning fog still clinging to the damp slopes. Somewhere in this wood was the quarry.

The man in front, feeling brave thanks to the morning sherry, his bolt-action Purdey, and the security man covering his back, was Lord Oakleigh. A Queen's Counsel lawyer of impeccable education, he had an impressive listing in *Debrett's* and his peer's robes were tailored by Ede & Ravenscroft. Oakleigh had long ago decided that these accomplishments paled in comparison to the way he felt now—this particular mix of adrenaline and fear, this feeling of being so close to death.

This, he had decided, was life. And he was going to live it.

The car had collected him at 4:00 a.m. He'd taken the eye mask he was given, relaxed in the back of the Bentley, and used the opportunity for sleep. In a couple of hours he arrived at the estate. He recognized some of his fellow hunters, but not all—there were a couple of Americans and a Japanese gentleman he'd never seen before. Nods were exchanged. Curtis and Boyd of The Quarry Co. made brief introductions. All weapons were checked to ensure they were smart-modified, then they were networked and synced to a central hub.

The tweed-wearing English contingent watched, bemused, as the Japanese gentleman's valet helped him into what looked like tailored disruptive-pattern clothing. Meanwhile the shoot security admired the M600 TrackingPoint precision-guided rifle he carried. Like women fussing over a new baby, they all wanted a hold.

As hunt time approached, the players fell silent. Technicians wearing headphones unloaded observation drones from an operations van. Sherry on silver platters was brought around by blank-faced men in tailcoats. Curtis and Boyd toasted the hunters and, in his absence, the quarry. Lastly, players were assigned their security—Oakleigh was given Alan, his regular man—before a distant report indicated that the hunt had begun and the players moved off along the lawns to the treeline, bristling with weaponry and quivering with expectation.

*   *   *

Now deep in the woods, Oakleigh heard the distant chug of Land Rover engines and quad bikes drift in on a light breeze. From overhead came the occasional buzz of a drone, but otherwise it was mostly silent, even more so the farther into the woods they ventured and the more dense it became. It was just the way he liked it. Just him and his prey.

"Ahead, sir," came Alan's voice, urgent enough that Oakleigh dropped to one knee and brought the Purdey to his shoulder in one slightly panicked movement. The woods loomed large in his crosshairs, the undergrowth keeping secrets.

"Nothing visible," he called back over his shoulder, then cleared his throat and tried again, this time with less shaking in his voice. "Nothing up ahead."

"Just hold it there a moment or so, sir, if you would," replied Alan, and Oakleigh heard him drop his assault rifle to its strap and reach for his walkie-talkie. "This is red team. Request status report…"

"Anything, Alan?" Oakleigh asked over his shoulder.

"No, sir. No visuals from the drones. None of the players report any activity."

"Then our boy is still hiding."

"It would seem that way, sir."

"Why is he not trying to make his way to the perimeter? That's what they usually do."

"The first rule of combat is to do the opposite of what the enemy expects, sir."

"But this isn't combat. This is a hunt."

"Yes, sir."

"And it isn't much of a hunt if the quarry's hiding, is it?" Oakleigh heard the note of indignation in his voice and knew it sounded less like genuine outrage and more like fear, so he put his eye back to the scope and swept the rifle barrel from left to right, trying to keep a lid on his nerves. He wanted a challenge. But he didn't want to die.

Don't be stupid. You're not going to die.

But then came the crackle of distant gunfire, quickly followed by a squall of static.

"Quarry spotted. Repeat: quarry spotted."

Oakleigh's heart jackhammered, and he found himself of two minds. On the one hand, he wanted to be in the thick of the action. Last night he'd even entertained thoughts of being the winning player, imagining the admiration of his fellow hunters, ripples that would extend outwards to London and the corridors of power, the private members' clubs of the Strand, and chambers of Parliament.

On the other hand, now that the quarry had shown himself capable of evading the hunters and drones for so long, he felt differently.

From behind came a rustling sound and then a thump. Alan made a gurgling sound.

Oakleigh realized too late that something was wrong and wheeled around, fumbling with the rifle.

A shot rang out and Alan's walkie-talkie squawked.

"Red team, report! Repeat: red team, report!"

CHAPTER 2

COOKIE HAD BEEN hiding in the lower branches of a beech. From the tree he'd torn a decent-sized stick, not snapping it, but twisting so it came away with a jagged end. Not exactly sharp. But not blunt, either. It was better than nothing.

He'd watched the player and his bodyguard below, waiting for the right moment to strike.

Forget the nervous old guy. He had a beautiful Purdey, but he was shaking like a shitting dog. The bodyguard was dangerous, but the moment Cookie saw him drop his rifle to its strap, he knew the guy was dead meat.

Sure enough, the guard never knew what hit him. Neither of the hunters had bothered looking up, supreme predators though they were, and Cookie dropped silently behind Alan, bare feet on the cool woodland floor. As his left arm encircled Alan's neck, his elbow angled so that his target's carotid artery was fat, his right arm plunged the stick into the exposed flesh.

But the years of drugs and booze and sleeping rough had

taken their toll, and even as he let Alan slide to the ground to bleed out in seconds, the old guy was spinning around and leveling his hunting rifle. And where once Cookie's reactions had been as fast as his brain, now the two were out of alignment.

Oakleigh pulled the trigger. Cookie had already seen that he was left-handed and knew how the weapon would pull, and so he twisted in the opposite direction. But even so, he was too slow.

He heard tree bark crack and saw splinters fly a microsecond before he heard the shot. A second later, pain flared along his side and he felt blood pool in the waistband of his jeans.

The stick was still in his hand, so he stepped forward and rammed it into the old guy's throat, cursing him for a coward, as Oakleigh folded to the ground with the stick protruding from his neck.

"Red team, report! Red team, report!" wailed the walkie-talkie. But even though Cookie knew others would be arriving soon, he needed a moment to compose himself, so he leaned against a tree, pressing his palm to the spot where the bullet had grazed him. He pulled up his sweater to inspect the wound. It looked bad, but he knew from painful experience it was nothing to worry about. Blood loss and the fact that he'd be easier to track were the worst of it.

He took stock. The old guy was still twitching. Alan was dead. Cookie reached for the security guard's assault rifle, but when he inspected the grip, he found it inset with some kind of sensor. His heart sank as he tried to operate the safety and found it unresponsive, knowing what the sensor meant: smart technology. Linked to the user's palm print. And if his guess was correct…

Fuck! The old guy's Purdey was equipped with the same. He tossed it away. From Alan he took a hunting knife. The old guy had a sidearm, also smart-protected and also useless.

The hunting knife would have to do. But now it was time to find out if these Quarry Co. guys were going to fulfill their part of the bargain. He put a hand to his side and started running. Leaves stung his eyes. Twigs lashed him. He stumbled over roots bubbling on the ground and reached to push branches aside as he hurtled forwards in search of sanctuary.

From behind came the crash of gunfire. Overhead, the sound of the drones intensified. They'd spotted him now. The time for stealth was over. He just had to hope he'd given them enough to think about in the meantime, and that the two casualties would slow them down.

Teeth bared, hatred in his bones, he kept running. The trees were thinning. Ahead of him was a peat-covered slope, and he hit it fast. Scrambling to the top, he was painfully aware that he'd made himself a visible target, but he was close now. Close to the perimeter.

"If you reach the road you win. The money's yours."

"No matter who I have to kill along the way?"

"Our players expect danger, Mr. Cook. What is the roulette wheel without the risk of losing?"

He'd believed them and, fuck it, why not?

And there it was—the road. It bisected a further stretch of woodland, but this was definitely it. An observation drone buzzed a few feet above him. To his left he heard the sound of approaching engines and saw a Land Rover Defender leaning into the bend, approaching fast. Two men in the front.

They didn't look like they were about to celebrate his victory. He tensed. At his rear the noise of the approaching hunting party was getting louder.

The Defender roared up to his position, passenger door flapping as it drew to a halt. A security guy wielding the same Heckler & Koch assault rifle carried by Alan stepped out and took up position behind the door.

"Where's my money?" called Cookie, with a glance back down into the basin of the woods. He could see the blurry outlines of players and their security among the trees, the crackle of comms. "You said if I reached the road I win," he pressed.

Ignoring him, the passenger had braced his rifle on the sill of his window and was speaking into a walkie-talkie, saying something Cookie couldn't hear. Receiving orders.

"Come on, you bastards. I reached the fucking road, now where's my money?"

The passenger had finished on the walkie-talkie, and Cookie had been shot at enough times to know the signs of it happening again. There was no prize money. No winning. No survival. There were just hunters and prey. Just an old fool and a man about to gun him down.

The passenger squeezed off bullets that zinged over Cookie's head as he tucked in and let himself roll back to the bottom of the slope.

I can do this, he thought. He'd fought in Afghanistan. He'd fought with the best, against the best. He could go up against a bunch of rich geriatric thrill-seekers and come out on top—security or no security. *Yes.* He was going to get out of this and then he was going to make the fuckers pay.

He could do it. Who dares, wins.

Then a bullet ripped the top of Cookie's head off—a bullet fired from a TrackingPoint precision-guided bolt-action rifle.

"Oh, good shot, Mr. Miyake," said the players as they emerged from the undergrowth in order to survey the kill.

They were already looking forward to the post-hunt meal.

CHAPTER 3

IT WAS DARK and Shelley was ground down after fruitless hours in various London shitholes, when trouble leaned on the bar.

It was the last place he'd intended to visit that day: the Two Dogs on Exmouth Market, a pub that was always open and always gloomy inside, forbidding to all but the early morning traders, afternoon postal workers from nearby Mount Pleasant Mail Center, and gangs of rail-link laborers who descended at nighttime.

Shelley had cast an eye across the gathered throng with a sinking heart, sensing he'd get no joy from this lot. Most were already half in the bag. They were likely to give him the runaround, just for the hell of it.

So, a wasted day. The only thing to say for it was that Lucy would be proud. They'd both known there was a danger he'd simply dig in at the first pub he visited, emerging a day later with a hangover and a bad case of drinker's guilt. But no. All temptation and even the odd invitation had been resisted. He'd done the rounds as sober as a judge. A man on a mission.

Word of which had evidently got around, if the guy leaning on the bar was anything to go by.

"You're looking for somebody, I hear?" he said now, with a voice that sounded like a cement mixer.

Shelley stared into rheumy, drink-sodden eyes and knew a shakedown when he saw one. After all, with his black woolen overcoat and baker-boy cap tilted rakishly, Shelley knew he stood out. That was the plan. But the same presence that made him a serious customer also made him a target for shakedowns and, from the looks of things, matey-boy here had in mind something more ambitious than a drink in return for yet more useless information. There was the knife he was wearing, for one thing.

"Yeah, I'm looking for someone," said Shelley, smiling.

"Your brother, is it?" rasped the drunk. He wore an Adidas tracksuit top zipped to the neck. He had an air of menace that was as distinctive and recognizable to Shelley as the smell of shit.

"No, he's not my brother. A friend."

Best friend, he thought. *Always got your back.*

"Brothers-in-arms, though, isn't it? You were in the forces together—you and this mate you're looking for."

That was interesting. The guy was unfazed by Shelley's background. Which meant either he was very stupid or he had backup somewhere.

Shelley leaned towards him. "You're right, mate. Yeah, we

served in the SAS together. Cookie and I were part of a covert three-man team operating in Afghanistan. We carried out assassinations, broke up kidnapping attempts, interrogated suspects. All three of us in the team were highly trained in surveillance, counterintelligence, situational awareness, and marksmanship. Each of us was expert in unarmed combat—a combination of Filipino Kali, Krav Maga, and Jeet Kune Do, with a bit of streetfighting thrown in for good measure, just because we liked it that way. We were anti-fragile. You know what that means? It means the worse shit gets, the more efficient you are.

"See, that knife you're carrying in the waistband of your jeans, Cookie would take a preemptive approach to it. And knowing him as I do, which is very well indeed, he'd use one of those beer glasses as a field-expedient weapon. He'd glass you, take the knife, and you'd be picking bits of beer bottle out of your throat while he was taking the piss out of you for not keeping your blade sharp enough.

"Thing is, Cookie was always a touch more reckless than me. Hit them first, hit them hard, and make sure they know they'd been hit, that was his motto. Me, I'm a bit more 'by the book.' I'd wait for you to draw the knife before I took it off you, and I'd break your arm doing it, *then* I'd take the piss out of you for not keeping it sharp enough.

"And so, knowing all that. Knowing now what you're dealing with here, how about you tell me any information you have? If it's useful, I can assure you I'll be grateful. Otherwise, you better take your knife and make yourself scarce before I get the wrong idea and decide to do things the Cookie way."

The drunk affected a hurt look. "Well, if you're going to be like that, you can shove it where the sun don't shine," he spat, then pushed himself off the bar and out of Shelley's orbit.

Shelley sighed and turned his attention to the barman, producing the same snapshot of Cookie that he'd shown at least a dozen barmen that day. The guy barely gave it a look before shrugging and moving away.

That shrug, it must be in the manual, thought Shelley. His eyes went to the mirror behind the bar and he watched the drunk skulk out of the door, thinking that he hadn't seen the last of that one.

He was right about that.

CHAPTER 4

HIS PHONE CHIRRUPED as he stepped out into the cold of Exmouth Market.

"Yeah?"

"Is that Captain David Shelley?"

"Been a while since anyone called me that."

"It's been a while since you left the SAS."

"Three years."

"It was two years ago that you left the SAS, actually. Two years, three months, and change, if we're being precise." The guy had a neutral voice, difficult to place. That would be deliberate. Shelley had wondered if his MoD request for the present whereabouts of Cookie (response: no fixed abode) might have triggered a flag at Whitehall. Maybe this was the flag waving.

"Well, you've got my attention. What do you want to know?"

"I hear you're looking for Major Paul Cook, your old commanding officer."

"Who is this?"

"Who I am can wait. You're going to have to bear with me on that. In the meantime, I have something I must tell you."

"He's dead, isn't he? Cookie's dead?" He'd been half expecting it, of course, but even so. Something inside him bunched up. He felt the kind of guilt and shame that might be banished by a drink, but he fought those conflicting emotions: the urge to drink, the grief.

"I'm sorry," said the caller.

"How? How did he die?"

"That's something we need to discuss. Are you by any chance within striking distance of the Chelsea and Westminster Hospital?"

"I can be."

"Can you go there now?"

"I can."

"Good. I'll make contact outside. Oh, Mr. Shelley? I need to know how long you'll be—as accurately as possible, please."

Shelley's gaze went to where the skeletal structures of market stalls disrupted the dark of Exmouth Market. Practiced eyes sought out hiding places and, sure enough, his Two Dogs trouble lurked in the shadows farther along.

"Make it an hour," he said.

"Very well. I'll see you then."

Shelley ended the call, then strolled in the direction of

Yardley Street until the guy from the pub appeared from the doorway of Greggs. Shelley stopped. Hands in his coat pockets, he gripped his phone.

"I thought we'd reached an understanding," he called. "You leave me be, I don't break any of your bones. Seemed fairly straightforward to me."

Moonlight skittered along the blade of the knife. "You like talking down to me, don't you?" said the guy. "You think I'm stupid."

"No, mate, I think you're desperate, and there's a difference. Look, final offer. Put the knife away and we'll say no more. I'll even spot you a drink. Maybe even one for your two friends behind me."

The guy's eyes widened. With the element of surprise lost, he seemed to consider, wondering if a drink wasn't such a bad return on the encounter. But his friends behind thought differently. They hadn't met Shelley. Hadn't experienced firsthand the aura of danger. And they made their move.

Shelley kept himself in shape, but there were certain habits he'd let slip since leaving the SAS. He no longer performed knuckle push-ups or punched bags of rice to keep his fists hard, so rather than risk his hand, he used the edge of his phone to break the first guy's nose.

The effect was instant: overwhelming pain, confusion, and blindness, his attacker neutralized at once. Shelley finished it. He grabbed a fistful of the guy's hair, drove an elbow into his temple, then dragged the limp body across himself to block the second assailant. This one had a knife, but Shelley jabbed into the guy's septum with the flat of his right hand. A little harder and he could have killed him. As it was, he simply put him down and then reached to scoop up the knife.

"Fuck's sake," he called after the guy from the pub, who had turned and shown a clean pair of heels, "you lot can't sharpen knives for shit."

CHAPTER 5

"CAPTAIN SHELLEY." THE man who stood beside a low wall outside the hospital wore a woolen coat and black jeans similar to Shelley's, almost as though he were deliberately mirroring him. "My name is Claridge," he said, and held out his hand to shake.

Shelley's eyes ran down the line of his coat, but he guessed if the guy was carrying a weapon, it would be better hidden than that. "You're MoD, are you?"

"No, MI5. Now, if you'd like to follow me inside, and follow my line exactly, please."

"It's like that, is it? We want to keep our TV appearances to a minimum."

Claridge nodded. He was about the same age as Shelley, both of them knocking on forty, but he was as neat and nondescript as his voice. "I've already been inside and paved the way, so to speak. We need to make the best use of our time, so any more talking we'll do in the mortuary."

They stepped inside the hospital, Shelley tracing Claridge's steps. As they descended to the mortuary he felt the old tickle of anticipation, then remembered why they were here: because Cookie was dead; because *I've always got your back* was suddenly an empty promise.

The mortuary attendant slept at his desk, and the department was otherwise empty. Claridge tutted as they passed, raising a wry eyebrow. "Fast asleep. And with all that coffee, too."

"How long will he be out?"

"Half an hour. It's all we'll need."

They passed through more double doors and into a room that was markedly colder. Claridge approached a bank of metal drawers, reaching for the one marked "Cook, P."

"The body was discovered behind bins in an alley at the back of Tottenham Court Road. A quantity of cocaine was found in his jacket pocket. The official line of inquiry is that your friend was involved in a drug deal that went wrong."

Cookie hated drugs, thought Shelley. *As far as he was concerned, they were the devil's business.* But of course a lot could change.

"Perhaps you'd like to suspend judgment until you see the body." Claridge hesitated, his hand on the drawer. "I must warn you, it's not pretty."

"He was never what you'd call an oil painting."

"I'm afraid he looks a lot worse now." Out came the drawer and right away Shelley noticed the unusual contours of the sheet covering the head. He nodded to Claridge, who drew the sheet down to the neck.

Shelley clenched his jaw. It was Cookie, but only just. Cookie, missing most of his skull, the brainpan like a jagged rocky outcrop, the cavity empty where what was left of the brain had been removed.

"The autopsy's been carried out?" he asked.

"I have a copy for you here." From his coat, Claridge produced a brown manila folder that he passed to Shelley.

Shelley leafed through, moving around the drawer to inspect the head wound. A thought made him catch himself. *It's not just another body on the battlefield—this one is Cookie.* Then he forced himself to return dispassionately to the matter at hand.

"No rim burn, it says here. No scorching or stippling on the wound. Means the shooter stood at a distance." He looked at Claridge. "What does that tell you?"

"I'm your standard-issue pencil-pusher. I want your opinion."

"It means your drug-deal-gone-wrong theory is most likely cobblers."

"It's not my theory."

"Any casings at the scene?"

"No."

"Any physical evidence of shots fired at the scene?"

"Not even any reports of shots fired."

Shelley examined the wound some more, glad that the body's eyes were closed. He referred back to the autopsy notes, talking to himself as much as Claridge. "No slug recovered, obviously."

Claridge shook his head. "What do you think we would have learned from it?"

"The slug? Well, it would depend if the weapon's riflings were on record. Otherwise, not a lot we can't work out from the wound. Damage like this, the slug had to come from a high-powered shoulder weapon and, with that kind of rifle, it doesn't matter if you hit anything major, because the shock or blood loss does the rest." He stopped. Thinking. "But this was a head-shot. This wasn't snatched in haste. The shooter took his time, fired from a distance. What kind of weapon do you choose for its stopping power *and* for long-distance capability?"

"It depends what you plan to shoot with it."

"A bloody elephant, by the looks of things." He shot a look at Claridge, only to see the MI5 man staring impassively back at him. Shelley drew back the remainder of the sheet, revealing the Y-shaped autopsy incision sutured to the groin. On Cookie's side was a bullet graze. Shelley consulted the notes. "A smaller caliber. Evidently fired in haste. This one left stippling, but no soot, which means it was fired from closer range, probably a few feet away. So this came first, the kill-shot second. Either the assailant winged him and then changed guns to finish the job, or there was more than one assailant.

"What clothes was he wearing when he was found?"

"It's in the notes. An anorak, jeans, sweater—none of it too fragrant. As you know, Major Cook was of no fixed abode. It appears he had been sleeping on the streets."

Shelley winced with a twinge of guilt. It had been over a year since he last spoke to Cookie. He'd tried Cookie's old phone and what turned out to be a mothballed email account, and he'd sent a card at Christmas. But scraping a living, setting up in business, life with Lucy—all that had got in the way of being there for his old CO, making sure his friend was okay, watching his back. Until one day Shelley woke up and it hit him how long it was since they'd last spoken, and the alarm bells had started ringing.

"Homeless then," he said. "And Scotland Yard gets a lot of homeless men killed in drug shoot-outs, does it?"

"Remember: not my theory."

"Stomach contents…he'd eaten well. Steak, potato. He always did love his steak and chips. No presence of alcohol or drugs. It's a strange kind of rough he was living."

Again he glanced at Claridge, who remained deadpan.

"Look at this," said Shelley, waving the report at Claridge. "There was no blood on his clothes. No damage consistent with his wounds. What does that tell us?"

"That he wasn't wearing those clothes when he died."

There was something about Claridge's voice that made Shelley glance over sharply. "That means something to you, does it?"

"It might. Maybe. I don't know. Continue," said Claridge.

"And look at these marks on his wrists and hands. Report says unidentified marks on the wrists, but that looks like handcuffs to me."

"You could have got out of those," said Claridge.

Shelley threw him a puzzled look. "What makes you say that?"

"You're double-jointed. It says so in your record."

Shelley frowned, then returned his attention to Cookie's hands, noticing patches of damaged skin. "Both of them have this…it's a burn of some kind."

He reached and placed Cookie's hands together, just as they would have been while handcuffed, and inspected the burns.

"It's as though he were holding something. Some kind of small explosion in his hands." He replaced Cookie's hands by his side. "It says there was a splinter, too."

"Yes, it was sent to the lab for testing," said Claridge. "It's since disappeared."

Shelley raised an eyebrow. "You don't seem surprised by that."

"I'm not."

CHAPTER 6

SHELLEY FOLLOWED CLARIDGE to an old BMW parked on a side street away from prying electronic eyes. Taking seats inside, they sat in silence for a moment or so.

"How did he get there?" asked Shelley, crippled with guilt that he didn't know the answer himself. "How did he end up on the streets?"

"He had a relationship breakup."

Susan, thought Shelley. He had never liked Cookie's girlfriend. Loud and coarse, and the kind of drug addict they called a garbage-head, who'd take anything as long as it got her high.

"He went traveling for six months," continued Claridge. "As far as we know, when he returned home he had been evicted from his flat in Hammersmith. Most homeless people assume theirs is a temporary situation, just until they get themselves sorted. You remember summer last year? Not a bad time to be sleeping out-of-doors. But the drink takes hold. One night under Waterloo Bridge becomes two weeks, then two months..."

"Then a year."

"Ten percent of all people living rough on the streets are ex–armed forces."

Shelley wondered where the MI5 guy was going with this, as Claridge picked up and handed him a newspaper folded to the headline *Lord Killed in Freak Hunting Accident*.

"This is two weeks old," said Shelley.

"The very same day Major Cook was killed, in fact."

"Just call him Cookie. He hated his rank. Couldn't stand being called Captain Cook. Didn't like Major Cook much better. *Major Cook, major stare.*" Shelley gave a short laugh as he remembered, picturing his friend's grinning face and using it to replace the dead one he'd just seen. "This Lord Oakleigh who died, what's he got to do with it?"

"Officially, Oakleigh accidentally shot himself while out hunting, but I've had sight of a suppressed autopsy report concluding that he was stabbed to death by an assailant, using a weapon improvised from a tree branch. I believe that assailant was Cookie."

"Right." Shelley took a deep breath. Instinct honed by years of service told him what was coming. "Okay. So there's an official version and there's an unofficial version. Why are you telling me the unofficial version?"

"I'm telling you because you were looking for Cookie and because I've seen your record. You're a company man, but a company man of integrity, and the two so rarely come as a package. On top of all that, you have tremendous field skills. You are, in short, exactly the operative I'm looking for."

Shelley's voice was hard. "Right, first, I'm *not* your operative. Nor am I a 'company man,' and I never was. I was a soldier, fighting for Queen, country, and the man at my side. And that's 'was,' in the past tense. Do you understand? I'm no longer a plaything for the likes of you to send somewhere unpleasant. I'm a guy who lives in Stepney Green with a wife and a dog, and a security consultancy business that won't quite get off the ground. A regular Joe, as the Yanks say. And the more I hear from you, the more I'm getting the nasty feeling that even sitting here is putting all that at risk."

The internal light flicked on as Shelley opened the door to go.

"You can avenge him," Claridge said quickly. "You can do this last thing for your friend."

Shelley closed his eyes. He felt as though his guilt were on show for Claridge to see.

"Listen, you're right," pressed Claridge. "This knowledge alone would be enough to get you killed. But I guarantee you this: when you hear the rest of what I have to say, if you're even half the soldier I think you are, you *will* want to take action; you won't be able to stop yourself from taking this job. What's more, I can see to it that you're amply rewarded. This security company you're trying to get off the ground, for example. I'm a section head at MI5, Shelley, I can see to it that a lot of business comes your way."

Shelley closed the door. He waited until the internal light dimmed and shut off before he next spoke.

"Tell me what you have to say."

CHAPTER 7

"I'M OFF THE books here, Shelley. There is no official capacity to this. I'm investigating an organization that…well, I don't even know if it is 'an organization,' as such, but I believe I know what it does. I have material suggesting that Lord Oakleigh and other players were fully aware they were taking part in a hunt using real guns and firing real bullets, with a human as prey."

"Players?"

"That's what they call themselves."

Shelley gave a short, disbelieving laugh. "This material—what is it?"

"It's a story that begins with one of the wives, and her husband taking an abnormal interest in his phone and computer. She overheard something about a meeting. At first she assumed he was having an affair. We were at Cambridge together, we were…*close* back then, so she came to me with her concerns, not as an MI5 operative, but as a friend. As a favor, I mounted a little surveillance work. What I saw was hubby meeting two smartly dressed men and discussing something over a laptop. I didn't recognize either of the men, but reported back about the meeting and thought little of it, relieved on her behalf that he was probably making some financial arrangements rather than cheating on her.

"But then she made contact again. There had been more calls, more secrecy; he was arranging to spend a weekend away, apparently on a golfing holiday, but the excuse he gave proved false when she checked it. With my friend's permission I hacked his phone, and it's lucky I did, because what I heard was that players were being swept for bugs. I got perhaps two minutes of rather vague conversation before all personal electronic devices had to be given up, and it didn't make for an edifying broadcast. They were discussing a hunt, with an SAS man as the quarry. I might have assumed it was some kind of paintball game, had I not heard the word 'kill-shot.'"

Shelley shrugged. "It could have been a euphemism."

"Of course. And that's what I hoped. But perhaps I heard something in their voices. Maybe it was just a whim. Either way, I decided to monitor recently deceased ex-SAS men. Two days after this phone call, Cookie's name came up. Having seen the body, you can understand why I reached the conclusion I did."

"Oh, come on. It's…insane."

"It is, yes. But tell me this. In your heart of hearts, does it *surprise* you? Does it really seem so far beyond the pale?"

Shelley's mind was on the weaponry and Cookie's wounds, thinking of Oakleigh and making connections. "Hunting," he said thoughtfully. "It was a hunting rifle that killed him…" He pieced together what he knew. "Oakleigh fired the smaller-caliber rifle. He was close to Cookie, must have thought he had the drop on him. He pulled the trigger, grazed Cookie. Cookie finished it. But then…then somebody else killed Cookie?"

"It would seem that way."

"Killed him with a hunting rifle. Sniper-shot."

Jesus, he was thinking, *of course. They hunted him down and picked him off.*

"They were definitely talking about a hunt?"

"They were. According to my friend, her husband has rekindled an interest in hunting, too."

"God! And that's it? That's where your investigation drew to a halt? What about the two guys you saw your friend's husband meet? I assume you've got some visual."

Claridge produced a picture on his phone. A grainy shot taken through the window of a lawyer's office. All three men were indistinct. .

"This all?"

"At the time it was all I needed, to put Sarah's mind at rest."

"What about CCTV?"

"Either by accident or design, they stuck to dead spots."

"Design, no doubt. They knew what they were doing. How about checking with appointments at the lawyer's office?"

"I hacked the computer. The identities of the two men signing in at that time turned out to be false. The trail is cold there, Shelley. I did everything I could do. In the meantime, I did some more checking. Cookie wasn't the first homeless ex-serviceman to die in similar circumstances. There were two incidents last year, also brushed conveniently under the carpet. It was around about then that it struck me just how far-reaching this thing could be."

"The body dumped in the street—it's deliberate flaunting," said Shelley thoughtfully, disgust in his stomach. "They could dispose of it, but they allow the bodies to be discovered as a way of publicizing the kill. It gives the players peace of mind. They get to see the cover-up happening in real time."

"Exactly. And the fact that they're able to do that points to a high-level conspiracy of silence. I have to assume that there are eyes on this at every level. Anything I do to draw attention to myself…" He tailed off, before adding, "To know more, I need someone on the inside."

"And you think that's me, do you?"

"I'm hoping."

"Well, you can stop hoping."

"Shelley, come on. Don't you want justice?"

"It's not that easy," said Shelley. "Even if I buy into your theory, there are other considerations, other responsibilities. I'm sorry, you're going to have to find another way."

Claridge gave a dry laugh. "What do you suggest I do? Send a group email to all of Thames House, Vauxhall Cross, and Parliament? 'Could anyone who doesn't hunt homeless men please get in touch?' You fail to see the problem, Shelley. The problem is I don't know who to trust within the intelligence community; the problem is finding someone I know is clean, and right now it's a straight choice between you and the postman. If the postman had your skills, I'd probably be talking to him."

"So conduct your own low-level investigation. Gather evidence. Do it the old-school way."

"I wouldn't last five minutes."

"Find a sympathetic journalist. Go public."

"I want to put a stop to this revolting practice, not bring this country to its knees. And that means no publicity, no public inquiry, no patsies taking the fall. It means giving these people a spanking they won't recover from."

"And you want me as chief spanker. An assassination job. Get inside and take out the two mystery men running the organization."

"Whatever you need to do. This is the blackest of black ops, Shelley."

"No. I'm sorry, but the answer is still no."

"Shelley, we need you."

"So does my wife. So does my dog."

Shelley opened the door and stepped out of the BMW.

"You won't be able to live with it," said Claridge. "You won't be able to live with knowing, and doing nothing about it."

"Well, fuck you very much for that, then," sighed Shelley, and slammed the door.

That night Shelley lay awake, with Lucy snoring gently beside him, his mind working overtime. He reached over to shake Lucy's shoulder.

She mumbled in her sleep.

"Lucy, wake up. There's something I need to ask you."

An hour later he called Claridge.

"Promise me this: if anything happens to me, you and your friend will see to it that Lucy is looked after?"

"You have my word."

"Then I'm in," said Shelley. "I'm in the game."

PART TWO

CHAPTER 8

THE HOMELESS MAN made his way along Commercial Street in Whitechapel, maintaining a discreet distance between himself and the thin-faced man he was following.

The thin-faced man went by the name of Colin. The homeless man answered to Steve, but had only used that name for the past four months. Before that he was Shelley.

Colin entered the Ten Bells, and Shelley stood with the smokers gathered outside, enjoying the fact that his presence made them nervous. He gazed through the window of the pub. Inside, Colin had met another man, this one a bit of a snappy dresser, complete with a tan leather jacket and a smart pair of Red Wing boots that Shelley couldn't help but admire.

He watched the snappy dresser sip from a pint, nodding and listening to Colin, who stood with his back to the window, preventing Shelley from being able to lip-read. Whatever it was that Colin was saying, it seemed to meet with the approval of the well-dressed man.

No doubt about it, in Shelley's mind: this was the next link in the chain.

As he stood there, Shelley caught sight of himself in the reflection on the window: old jeans; a pair of black leather loafers worn through; a sweater beneath a hooded; zipped-up jacket; and a scarf wound around his neck. His hair was lank and greasy, his cheeks sunken, a sprinkling of stubble. He looked the part, but that was just it—he was playing a role. He endured the constant nagging guilt of knowing that his appearance was a disguise, whereas Cookie had been living it for real.

"We know Cookie was registered with a night-center in St. Martin's and a Salvation Army hostel in Westminster," Claridge had said. *"According to the outreach workers who spoke to the police, he had the possibility of a studio flat in Wood Green. Now, I'm assuming that these people recruit under false pretenses, probably with the promise of a pay packet at the end of the hunt. Possibly Cookie wanted it for this flat, so that he could get back on his feet."*

"I'll need a new identity. Can you arrange that?"

Claridge came up trumps. *"From now on, you're Captain Steven Hodges, Royal Marine commando. He was deceased, but I've been able to un-decease him in your honor. He's the same age, same blood type, no photographs or fingerprints on record."* He handed over the record. *"Here, study this."*

It was the last time they'd met. Two days later, with his

new identity fully absorbed, Shelley had left his home in Stepney Green, kissing Lucy first and then Frankie the dog, before bidding them both good-bye, departing as David Shelley and entering a new life on the street as Captain Steve Hodges.

It was almost worrying how quickly he'd adapted. As Claridge had said, the streets were full of ex-servicemen, and they all liked to say that sleeping rough was nothing compared to bedding down in the freezing cold of an Afghan night. Shelley had to agree: Afghanistan was the most hostile environment he had ever known, roasting hot by day, bitterly cold by night, a terrain marked by razor-sharp rocks and stones and thistles that cut to the bone.

The difference was that in Afghanistan you were mostly all the same, whether you were bedding down in the scrub or in the relative luxury of a cot back at operating base. You weren't crouched beneath a bridge, trying to make a hobo stove and listening to the pop of champagne corks from a floating restaurant yards away. In the forces you looked out for your fellow man, it was practically the only reason you got up in the morning; you didn't step over him on your way out of the Tube station going to work. You didn't ignore him. It was that which made street life tougher than life in the forces. The men and women on the street sometimes liked to pretend there was a sense of solidarity, but they all knew it was dog eat dog. You were alone on the street. In the forces you could depend on two things: your friend was your friend, and your enemy was your enemy. Homeless, you fought on all fronts, not least the gnawing of your own soul.

After a couple of months, Shelley had got to know the street teams. These were volunteers who came out at night, checking on people's welfare and taking men and women to the shelters. Shelley took a bed in the St. Martin's shelter when he could, getting to know the street people. Watching, waiting, observing.

Now, after four months on the streets, he believed he'd identified a possible scout—a man he thought might be recruiting for the hunt. He was a rat-faced character by the name of Colin, who hung around the homeless and made a nuisance of himself at shelters. And he seemed particularly interested in a fellow named Barron.

Shelley had been aware of Barron for some time. Like Shelley, Barron hadn't been on the street for long. Unlike Shelley, he'd made his presence felt, constantly bragging about being an ex-Para. What was the old joke? *How do you tell a Para? You don't have to. He'll tell you.*

Barron was brawny. A bluebird tattoo peeped from under the collar of his hooded sweatshirt, and he was missing a couple of teeth. He was also, as far as Shelley could tell, a bully and a thug. Queue for the kitchen? Barron barged in. One cot remaining? That was for Barron. Pretty female volunteer? Barron was the one leering at her.

As well as letting it be known that he was an ex-Para, Barron had also been saying he was in line to make some easy money, that "certain people recognized talent when they saw it." He'd been boasting about it that very morning at breakfast.

"He wants to be careful, that one," the man Shelley was sitting next to had said.

"Oh yeah?" Shelley had replied. *"Why's that, then?"*

"Two of the men who got friendly with Colin ended up dead. That's all I'm saying."

That was more than enough for Shelley. It was time, he had decided, to have a word with Colin. He had stuck to Barron and, sure enough, Colin had turned up for a quick word at one of the day shelters. There was a noticeable change in Barron when Colin was around, as though his presence reminded Barron to be discreet. When Colin had left the day center, Shelley had followed.

Now Colin exited the Ten Bells and began to make his way back along Commercial Street. Shelley fell in alongside him.

"Hello, mate," he said.

Colin didn't break stride. "Yeah, mate, what can I do for you?" He wore a vinyl jacket and had a habit of shrugging his shoulders in it, like a man impersonating one of the gang members from *West Side Story*. He cast a sideways glance at Shelley. "Do I know you?"

"You might have seen me at the shelters."

"I see a lot of people at the shelters. What's on your mind?"

"I need to talk about Barron."

Colin blinked, and it was enough to give Shelley the satisfaction of knowing he was right.

"What about Barron?"

Mixing truth and lies, Shelley plowed on. "He says he's going to be making a bit of extra money, and it's got something to do with you. Says you recognize a man of talent."

"I might have a job for him—why?" said Colin, recovering his composure.

"I was thinking maybe I could do it better."

"And why might that be? You an ex-Para as well, are you?"

"Royal Marine commando. And I'm in much better shape than he is."

"Fuck me, this isn't a beauty contest, you know. Listen, mate, the position's taken. I'll bear your offer in mind. In the meantime, keep your mouth shut and your nose out of any business that doesn't concern you. Consider that a warning, okay?"

With that, Colin waved him off and sped away, leaving Shelley in his wake. Mission accomplished.

Shelley stopped, not really caring that pedestrians had to step around him. It suddenly occurred to him how close to home he was—close enough that he could be there in ten minutes, knocking on the door, kissing Lucy and cuddling Frankie. *"I just wanted to say hello. Just wanted to see your face..."*

For a moment or so the temptation to do it was almost overwhelming. But then he remembered that by talking to Colin he'd made himself visible. He was well aware that as soon as you popped your head over the parapet you made yourself a target. For all he knew, Colin could be making calls about him right now.

With a heavy heart he made his way back to St. Martin's. Usually he cut quite a figure on the street, even if he did say so himself. He had an eye for clothes; he looked good in a hat. But nobody checked him out now. There were none of the admiring glances from women that usually put a spring in his step. Other pedestrians looked through him or away, keen to avoid eye contact.

No matter. He had an appointment to keep.

CHAPTER 9

MIDDAY ON UPPER Street, Islington. Claridge drained the last of a McDonald's Sprite and then, in one surreptitious movement, eased off the lid and slid something inside.

Across the road he could see Shelley loitering outside the Tube station. He was unshaven, shabby, and a shadow of the man he'd first met, but still recognizably Shelley. The two made eye contact, but otherwise there was no sign they'd seen one another.

As Shelley crossed the road, Claridge dropped the McDonald's cup into a litter bin and turned smartly away. Shelley walked up to the bin, lifted out the cup, and moved off in the opposite direction.

He took a right onto White Lion Street, glanced to check he wasn't being followed, then flicked open the lid of the cup. What he saw inside made him tut: a micro-earpiece, which he extracted from the plastic wrapping and fitted into his ear.

"Hello? Shelley? Are you there?" Claridge was saying.

"What the bloody hell is this you've given me?"

"It's so we can talk."

"Christ, you can take the boy out of MI5, but you can't take MI5 out of the boy."

"You don't like it?"

"No. I need to see you."

"You don't need to see me."

"If I don't see you, how will I know you don't have a gun to your head? How do I know someone isn't listening in? You're MI5. I assume you know surveillance and evasion techniques. They still teach that, do they?"

"Well, I'm a little rusty, but—"

"Time to get un-rusty, Tin Man. In thirty seconds I'm stamping on this earpiece. Nine minutes and thirty seconds after that I'll meet you behind Trinity Church. Make sure you're not followed. Do it the old-school way."

Ten minutes later they sat together on a secluded bench at the rear of the church. Claridge shifted in his seat, nervously peering into the foliage that surrounded them on three sides.

"Have you made any progress?" he asked.

"I've identified the scout. A scumbag called Colin."

"Description? I'll see what I can find out—discreetly."

"Forget him, he's a single-celled organism. I'm more interested in his contact. No name yet, but it looks as though he conducts his business from the Ten Bells on Commercial

Street. See if you can check CCTV footage. Look for a well-dressed guy in a tan leather jacket, my height and age, neat dark hair, jeans, and good shoes. I'll work on getting more, but I've got something else I need to do first; this guy Colin and the snappy dresser—I'm 90 percent sure they have a mark in mind, a big-mouth ex-Paratrooper who uses the shelter, name of Barron. They'll have wanted to check Barron out. Could you find out who has accessed his records recently?"

"Maybe. How old do you think he is?"

"I've got about ten years on him."

Claridge drew breath sharply. "Well then, his records will be computerized, which makes accessing them a risk. I'd be logged, same as anyone else, and if there's a flag on the file—"

"Then don't open it."

"Are you sure? This is good detective work. It might be worth taking the risk."

"No, it's not. It's supporting evidence for when this is all over. You have family, don't you?"

"Yes."

"Then don't open the file. Not until we're done. Don't come to the meeting spot again, either. Don't try to contact me any other way."

"Why?"

"I'm going to take Barron's place. I'm going to be the quarry."

Claridge gave a start. "Are you sure?"

"Yes, of course." Shelley frowned. "And don't pretend that wasn't always the plan. How else was I going to penetrate this organization in any meaningful way?"

"I had hoped there might be more of a Trojan-horse aspect to it," said Claridge sadly.

"Impress them as a potential security man, you mean? Hope they're hiring, and then pray I pass whatever battery of security checks they have planned? Come on, you knew it had to go this way."

"It needed to be your decision. You're putting yourself in grave danger."

"At least this way I get to manage the danger. I don't have to worry about knowing whether they want to kill me or not. I *know* they want to kill me."

"Of course," said Claridge. There was a pause. "And we're understood that the objective is to put a stop to this."

Shelley nodded. "Which probably means killing the guys who organize it."

"We need to tie up loose ends."

Shelley barked a cynical laugh. "Well, yeah, of course. That'll be in everybody's interests, won't it?"

"I told you. The aim of this operation is to create a controlled explosion. A minimum of collateral damage."

"I'll see what I can do. In the meantime, I'll make contact if I can, but otherwise, forget about me and wait. My identity remains in place?"

"Of course."

"How were you able to set that up without being logged?"

"Well, that's where your relatively advanced age comes in handy."

Shelley shot him a look.

"*'Relatively,'* I said. Anyway, what it means is that it's a paper record. One from the pile marked 'to be digitized.' Old school, you see."

"And the player's wife? The one who alerted you to all of this?"

"She's being kept informed."

"Is she, indeed? Why do I get the impression she's well connected?"

Claridge chuckled. "And why do I get the impression you did a little checking on me, before you embarked on this mission?"

"Enough to find out who you studied with at Cambridge."

"Then you'll know that in Sarah we have a strong ally."

"Okay. You tell her I'm close."

Claridge nodded. "So what happens now?"

"I don't know. I'm hoping I'll think of something."

CHAPTER 10

THE HOME SECRETARY, Sarah Farmer, and her husband paid little attention to their television, even though it was on. Both were engrossed in other pursuits: Sarah was peering at papers spread on the coffee table in front of her, face bathed in the glowing light of her laptop screen; Kenneth was sprawled on the second sofa, his MacBook open, angled away from her.

"Have you noticed we never actually watch anything anymore?" she said.

"What was that, dear?"

"We're always working, looking at our computers. What is it that's got your attention?"

His eyes appeared over the aluminum lid. Eyes she once knew well. Now she wondered if she ever knew Kenneth at all. If what Simon thought was true, she had married a monster.

"Oh, nothing really," he said. "Nothing to interest you."

"It's not hunting equipment again, is it?" she said sternly, knowing it would be. Kenneth had taken to deleting his internet history and was in the habit of finding an excuse to slap his MacBook shut whenever she could see it. But the other day she'd caught him looking at telescopic sights on his laptop, the way other men looked at porn. "I realize you had to give up hunting after I was elected, dear—"

"Well, I had no choice." He scowled through an instant fog of resentment. "It wouldn't have done for your public image, would it?"

"And I'm very grateful. I hope the rewards have made it worthwhile."

He acknowledged the point with a petulant frown.

"So I hate to see you torturing yourself this way. Besides, it's golf that keeps you busy now, isn't it? You've been doing a lot of that lately."

She wondered if she sounded as disingenuous as she felt. *Hunting equipment.* God! She'd always known that her ascension to the post of Home Secretary would involve discovering some dark and unpalatable truths. She could never have imagined how repellent they were, or how close to home they would lie.

How ironic that she'd suspected him of an affair. Right now, she'd happily settle for that.

An instant-messaging bubble appeared on her laptop screen: ":-)" sent by "SC." Simon Claridge.

With a click of the trackpad she dismissed it and stood.

"Tell you what," she said to Kenneth, trying to sound affectionate, "you look at hunting sites all you want."

"That's very good of you, I must say, to allow me to look at the websites of my choice. Far be it from you to treat me like your personal puppet, eh?"

God, she thought. Who had taken the man she married and replaced him with this…*person?* If he was caught for this business, would he blame it on her—on her career?

With a heavy heart she stood. "I need to make a private call, Kenneth. State business."

"You have my blessing," he said sardonically as she left, closing the door behind her.

In the hallway, her protection officer scrambled to his feet, giving her a slight start. Even after two years in office, she still wasn't accustomed to finding an armed man in her hallway.

She was assigned two protection officers and a driver. Simon had looked into the detail, but he had to admit that he had no idea who was tainted and who was not. Gut instinct told him that some were good men. Others he was less certain about, the one in her hallway being one of them.

"Evening, ma'am."

"Evening, Harvey."

"I'm just going to use the phone in my office," she said.

"It's clear. I've just this second swept it," he told her.

She thanked him, stepped into her office, and retrieved a

mobile phone from her handbag on the desk. This was the phone she used for talking to Simon. Just Simon. She dialed him, so that he could bring her up to speed on any developments.

Meanwhile, outside in the hallway, the door to the lounge opened and the Home Secretary's husband peered into the corridor. He caught the eye of the protection officer, gave him a nod, and then disappeared back inside.

The protection officer moved to the office door. From his trouser pocket he produced a listening device that he suckered to the wood, adjusting his earpiece in order to hear one side of the Home Secretary's conversation.

CHAPTER 11

IT WAS FOOLHARDY and went against his own instructions, but he couldn't bear not hearing her voice. So, after ensuring he wasn't being watched, he let himself into one of the last remaining working phone boxes in the whole of the United Kingdom and called her.

"Hello," she said.

The stink of piss in the phone box was almost overwhelming, but the sound of her voice transported him home, and he bit back a surge of emotion.

"Lucy," he said.

"Oh, my God. Shelley, it's you. Are you okay?"

"It's Afghanistan without the IEDs."

"That bad?"

"And worse without you or Frankie. How are you both?"

"I'm all right. Daytime, I'm trying to keep the business ticking over. I think this is the first time I've ever been glad of the lack of business. Evenings, I'm dividing my time between bouts of worrying about you, *Game of Thrones*, and Frankie."

He didn't want to ask about the business. The sole up-side of this whole venture was that he was temporarily released from worrying about the business. Then again, he realized with a jolt of shame, all that worry was now trans-ferred to Lu.

"I'm sorry," he told her. "I'm sorry to put you through all this."

"Just tell me it's not out of guilt."

"It's not out of guilt. It's what's right."

"Nothing to do with the fact that you think it could have been you in Cookie's shoes?"

"I told you, it's—"

"There are different sorts of guilt, Shelley. Guilt for some-thing you did or didn't do; guilt because you didn't help someone. Survivor guilt; guilt because your wife chose you over your best friend."

He squeezed the receiver tight. In the background their kitchen radio played.

"He understood, you know," she said quietly. "He gave us his blessing."

"Do the same for me now, Lucy. Let me do this thing knowing I have your support."

"You don't have to ask for it. It's there, always. Do what you have to do. Just come back in one piece."

CHAPTER 12

FOR THE NEXT two days Shelley stuck to Barron like glue. He wasn't kidding when he told Claridge he didn't have a plan, and time was wasting away.

Then, that morning, shortly before the center was due to close for the day, his chance came.

Most of the nighttime residents had shambled away. Among those last to leave were Shelley and the man he was shadowing, who throughout breakfast had been telling anybody unfortunate enough to be in the dining room that "today's the day I'm going to earn some serious wonga."

His announcement sent Shelley's mind racing. Did that mean the hunt was today? Either way, he had to make his move.

The volunteer ushered out an aging woman named Josie, who shuffled out of the door, muttering. Meanwhile, a venerable old Indian man they called Raj was gently roused from his sleep and invited to be on his way.

Barron still hadn't moved. He sat at the table and made a show of licking his plate. Shelley decided to wait outside, so he shouldered his backpack and made his way to the street, where vehicles lined the sidewalks and warehouse conversions rose on both sides. Colin stood leaning on the bonnet of a parked car, arms folded. At the sight of Shelley he frowned. "What are you doing here?"

Shelley jerked a thumb back at the shelter. "Slept there last night," he said.

Behind him, the door opened and Barron appeared, belongings in hand.

"Aha," he rasped on seeing Colin, "my carriage awaits."

The moment hung. Shelley opened his mouth, knowing he had to say something or forfeit his only chance to muscle in on Barron. But Colin spoke first and gave him just the opening he needed.

"Here, Barron"—Colin leered— "our friend here was trying to put you out of a job the other day, so he was."

Barron's smile faded as he looked across to Shelley. "Oh yeah? Funny, now you come to mention it, he's been hanging round like a bad smell these past couple of days."

The tinted window of a black minivan parked on the other side of the street glided down noiselessly. In the passenger seat sat the snappy dresser Shelley had seen in the Ten Bells. He wore shades, his expression unreadable as he gazed across to where Barron was rounding on Shelley.

"So what makes this one think he can take my job, hey?" the bigger man was demanding to know.

Mouth split into a grin, Colin goaded him. "Says he's a commando. Said something about how Royal Marines eat Paras for breakfast."

"Did he now?" said Barron, pulling himself up to his full height and towering over Shelley, who didn't budge. His hands were in his coat pockets and he flexed them surreptitiously, careful to keep his features blank.

"I didn't say that," he said. "I didn't say Royal Marines eat Paras for breakfast."

"Good. You better not have, because—"

"But it's true. Royal Marines do eat Paras for breakfast."

Colin chortled in appreciation. Framed in the window of the minivan, the snappy dresser removed his sunglasses. An indignant Barron poked at Shelley, who allowed himself to be propelled back a few steps, using the opportunity to adjust his footing, withdrawing his hands from his pockets at the same time. His pulse quickened. His muscles bunched and tensed as Barron bore down on him, growling, "How about you put your money where your mouth is?"

The fight was on. But by coming close, Barron had sacrificed his only advantages—his height and reach—and when he threw a straight right, Shelley blocked it and responded with a left overhand punch, keeping his elbow bent and his chin tucked into his shoulder. Shelley felt Barron's jaw crack.

Colin gave an impressed whistle. Meanwhile Barron re-gained his footing, wondering how he'd failed to make contact. His eyebrows knitted in confusion, his brow darkened with fury, and he was drawing himself up, about to launch a second attack, when there came a whistle from the minivan.

"Does somebody want to tell me what's going on?" called the snappy dresser. His voice was neutral like that of Clar-idge. Another civil servant? Somebody high up in security?

From the way Barron assessed the new arrival, Shelley could tell it was the first time he'd clapped eyes on him, too. And that he instinctively realized this man was in charge.

"This joker's about to get a beating," Barron called back.

Colin, enjoying himself, pushed himself off the car and called back to his boss. "We've got a new contender for the position, guv," he said. "Bit of a cockfight going on about it."

Barron reddened and went into damage limitation. "Wait a minute. Wait a fuckin' minute—there's no competition for the position here. All we have is a Marine with ideas above his station."

The boss man called Colin over, they conferred, and a mo-ment later the rat-faced man jogged back. "Get in the car, both of you."

Barron shot a searing look at Shelley, but the minivan doors were opening and two stereotype gym bunnies in black leather jackets were stepping out and making their presence felt. Shelley had a history with men like that: shaved heads knew their way around a fight.

He and Barron were directed inside the car, sandwiched between the two heavies, who pointedly opened the windows to direct their noses outside. The snappy dresser turned to address Shelley. "Name?"

"Hodges. Captain Steve Hodges."

"You know Krav Maga, I see."

"A little," replied Shelley. "I learned in the commandos."

Barron sneered, but the boss man silenced him with a look and addressed Shelley again. "Where are you from?"

"Hampshire," replied Shelley. It was Steve Hodges's birthplace.

"Regiment?"

Again he supplied the dead man's details.

"Commanding officer?"

Shelley gave the name, but the leader shrugged with a grin. "Well, I'll have to take your word for that." He turned his attention to Barron. "What about you? Any martial arts up your sleeve?"

"I kick ass, is what I do," snarled Barron in reply.

The leader grinned, then faced forward and indicated for the driver to move. "We'll see about that in a moment or so, my friend," he said. "We'll see about that."

CHAPTER 13

DURING THE JOURNEY, the leader attended to his phone and Shelley guessed his details were being checked. Meanwhile, he decided that the two leather-jacketed bouncer types were twins. When they pulled up at an abandoned brewery warehouse, one had jumped out to haul open huge double doors. The minivan drove inside and the doors were closed behind them.

Inside, what feeble light there was fell through broken windows onto a concrete floor strewn with litter and debris. Looking up, Shelley saw crumbling gantries, a mezzanine floor, and walls daubed with graffiti. Water dripped through a huge gash in the roof high above them, and the slamming doors of the minivan disturbed birds that panicked in the rafters.

Their voices echoed in the cavernous space as the four men led Shelley and Barron towards the pool of light more or less in the center of the floor.

"Bag," said the snappy dresser, holding out his hand for Shelley's knapsack.

Before Shelley had embarked on the mission, Claridge had expressed surprise that he planned to go undercover without a single means of communication. Claridge had even suggested that they sew a mobile phone into the fabric of his knapsack. But as he watched his bag being expertly rifled by one of the twins, the search turning up nothing more incriminating than his sweater, a copy of the *Daily Mirror*, and a bread bag containing a few crusts, Shelley was doubly glad he'd stuck to his guns.

"Clean," said the twin, dropping Shelley's bag to the ground.

The snappy dresser nodded and turned his attention to Shelley. "Right," he said in his neutral, civil-service tones, "I know all about Sergeant Barron here, but you're a new contender, is that right?"

Barron bristled. One of the twins silenced him with an upraised finger and a practiced bouncer's stare.

Shelley nodded and the leader continued, "My name is Tremain. Colin here works for me, and I in turn work for an organization that arranges what you might call 'games.' Diversions, so that our client base can get away from their wives and let off a little steam during the weekends. We're called The Quarry Company, and for our customers we represent an alternative—an alternative to golf, or motor-racing, or stuffing themselves into Lycra and clogging up country roads on their bicycles, or organizing law-flouting fox hunts, or snorting coke off call girls. This is news to you as well, isn't it, Sergeant Barron?"

"Sounds good to me," snarled Barron. "Tell me what to do and when I can start, and let me get on with it."

"Well, that all depends on the outcome of this particular encounter."

Once again Shelley sensed the indignation pouring off Barron and almost felt sorry for the man. Up until twenty minutes ago he'd been cock of the walk, anticipating a payday. Suddenly he was in danger of being usurped. True, he was a scumbag; it couldn't happen to a nicer guy. But even so, Shelley felt bad for him, especially knowing what he knew, which was that only one of them would be allowed to leave the warehouse alive. There were no winners or losers here, just two losers.

"One of the most popular activities organized by The Quarry Company is a game based on the paintball model," Tremain was saying, "where we turn an experienced survivor loose in woodland terrain and our customers, bless their hearts, can experience the thrill of hunting human prey. Make no mistake: it's proper sport. We encourage a *visceral* edge to the hunt."

"Is he allowed to fight back, this quarry?" asked Barron, saving Shelley the trouble.

"Indeed he is. The quarry's objective is to survive. If he can reach a final flag, he wins himself a sizable sum in addition to what we're already paying him."

"And what are you paying?" asked Barron.

"Ten thousand," said Tremain. "Plus the same again if you can make it to the flag at the perimeter."

"So that's it?" Barron was unable to keep the excitement and greed out of his voice. "I just have to avoid getting shot at with paint by a bunch of toffs, crack a couple across the jaw, and collect my reward at the end of it?"

"Exactly. What do you think of that, Captain Hodges?"

Shelley needed to be careful, but didn't want to appear as credulous as Barron. "I think that in order to make decent sport, it might be a little more difficult than this guy thinks it is."

Tremain nodded. "Our players pay a lot of money in order to experience life on the edge, and we'd be failing in our duty if we didn't have something up our sleeves—something to differentiate our experience from the average stag party. Put simply, we have surprises in store for both sides. It's why we have to provide the management with a constant supply of new quarry, in order to keep the games fresh and the surprises surprising. Any questions so far?"

They shook their heads.

"In that case, we should let the selection process begin. Don't get too badly hurt now, will you?"

"What do you expect us to do?"

Tremain chuckled. "I expect you to fight. Winner takes all."

CHAPTER 14

STRAIGHTAWAY BARRON WHEELED and threw a right, but Shelley anticipated it and stepped smartly to the side. His hips snaked as he whipped his head away and heard the whistle of Barron's punch as it sailed past his head, and then he countered with a short and nasty extended-knuckle jab to Barron's groin.

The breath came out of Barron in a whoosh. For a second he was almost bent double and his eyeballs rolled upwards.

"Strike one!" called Colin with a short round of applause. The twins chuckled. Tremain stood with his arms folded, impassive.

Barron squeezed his eyes shut, trying to dismiss the pain. Shelley feigned being off-balance, knowing he could have stepped forward and followed up the jab with a closing punch, but not wanting to make his victory too quick. He needed to best Barron, but not easily enough to raise the Quarry men's suspicions.

Barron drew himself up, raising his fists in a boxer stance.

Shelley took up position, Krav Maga style, doing it for Tremain's benefit.

"Watch it, Barron," jeered Colin, "he's about to get all Bruce Lee on you."

With a shout Barron lumbered forward and Shelley decided to finish him. But this time he underestimated his opponent. Everything about Barron so far had said street-scrapper, but he had some boxing smarts and dipped his left shoulder, throwing a feint that Shelley fell for, hook, line, and sinker.

Bang! The right hook came fast and from nowhere and caught Shelley clean on the temple—hard enough to knock him to his knees on the warehouse floor. He was too dazed to stop what happened next, as Barron did what Shelley, foolishly, had failed to do, taking full advantage of his opponent's incapacity and following up fast.

Again. *Bang!* Shelley's vision went black as Barron threw a left that caught him above the bridge of the nose. A vicious kick to the ribs sent him sprawling.

He cursed his own stupidity, pledged not to make that mistake again, and then slapped his hands to the ground to stand. Above him, Barron had turned away, thinking himself victorious.

"There," he was saying to the Quarry men, "I think you'll find that settles it."

"No, I don't think so, Sergeant Barron. Your opponent has a little fight left in him yet," said Tremain.

Barron turned back.

"No ribs broken, I hope, Captain Hodges?" called Tremain. "Is the nose all right?"

"Here, hold up," protested Barron. "It's me you should be worried about."

"Oh, I am indeed worried about you, Sergeant Barron. Your opponent looks extremely upset."

Shelley hated himself for what he had to do next. As well as providing Tremain and company with their sport, he was sending Barron to his death. And though Barron was a scumbag, he was still a down-on-his-luck human being and he didn't deserve this.

There was nothing Shelley could do about that—nothing except make it easier for him.

The bones of the cranium take almost two years to fuse together from birth. As a result, there are particular areas that stay vulnerable for an adult's entire life. An index and middle finger jabbed at the precise spot induces instant unconsciousness. You have to know exactly where and exactly how hard; you have to know exactly what you're doing. Fortunately, Shelley knew what he was doing.

It wasn't a move he wanted to show the four Quarry men, so he danced around a little, bringing Barron's back to them before throwing his punch. Aiming at the side of Barron's head, Shelley's fist became a two-fingered jab, striking the spot precisely. Barron took three unsteady steps backwards and then, as his eyeballs rolled back once again, sank messily into the concrete.

The Quarry men looked at Barron, until it was beyond doubt that he was unconscious.

Tremain looked up at Shelley. "Well, that really is that, then. I hereby declare the selection process at an end. Congratulations, Captain Hodges."

Shelley indicated towards Barron. "What happens to him?"

"Oh, don't worry about him. When he comes round we'll see that he's adequately recompensed. Who knows? Perhaps your paths will cross at some point in the future. Now, I hope you have no objection to us whisking you away right now?"

His expression politely dared Shelley to object.

Shelley shook his head.

"Excellent. If you'd like to step into the car. Colin, if you wouldn't mind staying here and taking care of Sergeant Barron, that would be most appreciated."

Colin's eyes glittered. *At least the unconscious Barron would know nothing about it,* Shelley thought. He climbed into the car, taking a seat beside one of the twins.

The other leaned in and Shelley saw the jet injector in his hand.

"Arm," the twin said and Shelley did as he was told, baring his arm.

This is it, he thought as the injector gun came close to

him. He had no idea what would happen next. No idea if he'd have an opportunity to alert Claridge. No idea if he'd even wake up from the injection they were about to give him. All he knew for sure was that there was no turning back.

He belonged to The Quarry Company now.

CHAPTER 15

SOME DAYS LATER, Claridge was at home. His wife and two daughters were in another part of the house, playing Scrabble—or, if what Claridge had witnessed was typical of the game, mainly cheating at Scrabble. He'd taken the opportunity to creep away, installing himself at his office iMac.

He googled for a while, then made more checks. "Christ!" he muttered, then opened his messenger application and sent an IM: ":-) SC".

As he sat waiting for Sarah's call he thought of her and wondered if she ever regretted breaking up with him all those years ago, only to end up with Kenneth.

Claridge had never liked Kenneth. Of course that antipathy was in the process of being entirely vindicated, but back then neither of them could have known what darkness lay within Kenneth Farmer.

What turns a man that way? wondered Claridge. *What corrupted Kenneth?*

Money, perhaps? Kenneth certainly had a lot of that. Even

so, Claridge wondered how Kenneth was able to go toe to financial toe with the likes of Lord Oakleigh or the captains of industry that Claridge was convinced were involved. For something like this, the figures involved would be astronomical.

Maybe Kenneth was able to offer them something in addition to the money, or in place of it? He was, after all, husband to the Home Secretary and had bankrolled her political career. What influence might he wield? Claridge shivered at the thought.

His phone rang. "Hello, Simon," said Sarah. "You have news?"

"I do. You'll recall our agent was going dark, and that he hoped to be picked as the quarry."

"I do. But presumably there is no way of knowing when that happens?"

"The last time I spoke to our agent he mentioned he might have to gazump another man for the job, a Sergeant Philip Barron, previously of the Paratroopers."

"Yes?"

"A vagrant by that name was found stabbed to death by the docks the day before yesterday. It looked as though he was beaten up beforehand."

"You think our man did this?"

"If he did, then he would have had no other choice, Sarah."

"I see. So if he's in place, what now? What can we do?"

"There's nothing we can do, I'm afraid. We assumed he'd be thoroughly searched for any kind of surveillance device, so he doesn't have anything on him. His instructions are for us to wait."

"Wait for what?"

"That remains to be seen."

"Then God help him," she said.

"If he's as good as his record indicates, God help them all."

Outside in the corridor, the Home Secretary's security pushed down his sleeve and replaced his biro in his inside pocket, moving away to retake his position by the front door.

On the inside of his wrist he had written the word "Simon."

CHAPTER 16

SIR ERIC APPLEBY, Permanent Under-Secretary at the Foreign and Commonwealth Office, was striding purposefully across the lawn in the direction of the Commons when his phone rang.

Not long ago he'd gotten the hang of programming his phone so that callers had different ringtones, something he was disproportionately proud of having mastered. His teenage daughter had even awarded him an impressed high five. In return, he was able to screen calls from her and her mother with even greater ease. He didn't even need to look at his phone to ignore them.

Now, however, the hunting horn ring told him it was somebody else entirely—somebody it would not do to ignore. He stopped and, casting a quick look around to ensure there was nobody within earshot, took the call.

"Hello," he said.

"Voiceprint protocol, please, sir," came the reply. "State your name, if you would."

"Appleby."

"And your keyword, sir."

"Steeplechase."

There was a short pause, then he heard an electronic click. In the distance the Thames shimmered, and across the lawn the Chief Whip was being pursued by a pair of underlings. The two men exchanged a wave, and Sir Eric wondered if his colleague knew anything of "The QC," as it was called by those in the know.

"Sir Eric, hello. This is Curtis. Your voiceprint ID check is complete. I hope we find you well."

He felt his pulse quicken. "You do, Mr. Curtis, thank you very much. You're calling with news of an event, I take it?"

"Indeed, Sir Eric, at a premium location. Our head of security informs me that the quarry is an experienced combat veteran with an excellent record. As a result, this event is open to Gold Club members only."

Sir Eric swelled with pride. Attaining the experience points needed to rise to Gold Club status with the Company had been a high point of his life so far.

"Well, I must say I'm honored to be considered a part of the enterprise," he replied. He was simpering a little, he realized, but then again it couldn't hurt to keep on their good side.

"And we're grateful for your custom, Sir Eric. Our coming event is planned for the weekend after next. How does that sound?"

"I shall need to consult my diary," replied the Under-Secretary, knowing his decision already: whatever was diarized for that day would have to be rearranged.

"Of course, sir. Shall we say 1500 hours for your second call?"

"I'll have an answer for you by then."

"And, as is the usual procedure, a bid, too, if you please."

"Certainly."

"It's likely to be our last hunt of the season, Sir Eric; we intend to lay on some superb entertainment afterwards. Entertainment of a very willing and Russian persuasion. As you can imagine, we're anticipating a lot of interest from Gold Club members. Bidding begins at a minimum of three million, I'm afraid."

Appleby drew a large intake of breath.

"As ever, you have one opportunity to register your bid," continued Curtis. "Only winning bids will be notified. All notifications to be made by 0800 tomorrow."

"Perfect. I shall make myself available at three."

"Good speaking to you, Sir Eric."

Financial recruitment specialist Stuart Cowie was carrying an ancient, brick-sized mobile phone to a *Wolf of Wall Street* fancy-dress screening when his phone—his regular phone—rang.

Excited at the ID that flashed up on the screen, he answered quickly and then gave his name and voiceprint password, "Jerusalem."

"No," he said, when his caller had finished speaking, "you don't have to ring later, Mr. Boyd. My answer is yes and my bid is four."

There was a pause at the other end of the line.

"Hello?" prompted Cowie.

"We usually prefer our clients to consider bids and availability more carefully. These things really shouldn't be rushed, Mr. Cowie."

Emboldened by the line of coke he'd snorted from his desktop not twenty minutes ago, Cowie was excited; his blood was up. "Make it five, then," he said rashly.

"Thank you, Mr. Cowie. You will be informed whether or not your bid has been successful by 0800 hours tomorrow."

"At five million quid, it better bloody well be accepted," spluttered Cowie.

In the five-star Chiltern Firehouse, the German CEO of the defense company Diamond & Perry, Daniel Kiehl, was lunching with city lawyer Sebastian Bramwell.

Bramwell's phone trilled and, after shooting an apologetic look at Kiehl, he took the call. Listening, he said, "Bramwell. Shortcut," and then the number three. He ended the call, avoiding Kiehl's gaze as he replaced the phone on the tabletop and then resumed his conversation.

Nothing passed between the two men until, suddenly, Kiehl's own phone rang and, with an apology to Bramwell, he answered.

"Kiehl. Retinue," he said, and at that Bramwell gave a start, staring across the table at his dining companion, suddenly aware of what Kiehl had also just realized: they were both Quarry Company clients.

"Four," said Kiehl, with a "what can you do?" shrug for Bramwell.

The lawyer fumed.

Later, as their meal drew to an end, Kiehl's phone rang once more. Ignoring Bramwell's searching look, he answered, passing voiceprint ID again. Bramwell bared his teeth in frustration, peering at his own phone as though willing it to ring with the good news. His misery was complete when Kiehl said, "Thank you, Mr. Curtis," and ended the call.

"Next time, Bramwell, perhaps you will be fortunate," said Kiehl.

In the home of Sarah Farmer, the Home Secretary watched with interest as her husband left the room to take a call.

When he returned he was in an ebullient mood, kissing the top of her head before sitting back on the sofa and burying himself in his MacBook.

She churned with helplessness, hatred, disgust, and fear.

CHAPTER 17

SHELLEY WASN'T SURE whether he'd woken up or regained consciousness, but either way he found himself lying on a comfortable bed between clean and crisp sheets, in a room that was bright and smelled fresh.

He was wearing white boxers, not his own, but otherwise was just as he had been the day before. Whoever had gone to the trouble of changing his underwear had obviously stopped short of giving him a bath into the bargain. Very sensible. Hanging from the handle of a built-in wardrobe opposite the end of the bed was a faded-blue set of overalls, and on the carpet stood a new pair of Dr. Martens boots. Those, he guessed, would be his uniform for the duration of his employment with The Quarry Company.

So this was it, he thought, pulling himself out of bed. This was where they brought the quarry ahead of the hunt. No doubt where they'd brought Cookie. According to the autopsy report, there had been no ethyl glucuronide in Cookie's system, which meant no alcohol. And by Shelley's reckoning, that indicated Cookie was dry for at least three days before he was killed, maybe four.

Three days of eating steak and drying out. The equivalent of fattening the goose for Christmas.

He found the bathroom. Again, it was clean and bright, the fittings virtually new. Then he explored the rest of what turned out to be a small but well-appointed one-bedroom apartment. He came to the conclusion that he was being kept (and to what extent he was being "kept," he wasn't yet sure) in an old holiday camp chalet, complete with a small dining area, bedroom, kitchen, and bathroom.

He peered out of the front window. Opposite were the gray, dilapidated buildings of what he took to be other chalets, complete with smashed windows, graffiti tags, and guttering that hung off at angles. Most surprising was the contrast of outside to inside. When he opened the front door he saw that the exterior of the door was as neglected as those opposite. The inside? Like a show home.

Somebody had gone to an awful lot of trouble here.

He heard the sound of a vehicle approaching. Alerted perhaps? He scanned the living area and saw a smoke detector in the ceiling. Camera in there, probably. Somewhere there were people watching his every move. And now they were coming for him.

Had it begun? Was this it? Whatever they used to knock him out would still be in his system. If it came to a fight, his reaction time would be reduced. His cognitive abilities, diminished.

Otherwise he was ready for them. No, not quite ready. He returned to the bedroom and pulled on the overalls. *Now* he was ready.

Footsteps on the walkway outside came closer. Then there was a knock at the door.

"Captain Hodges?" came a female voice. "Captain Hodges, are you decent?"

"I think you know very well I'm decent," he said.

"May I come in?"

"Of course."

She stepped in from the walkway outside. She carried a small suitcase and wore hospital whites, dark hair pulled into a ponytail. She was younger than him, maybe midthirties, and beautiful, with dark hair slightly graying at the temples framing a heart-shaped face and full lips, which he soon learned were in the habit of breaking out into a wide, impish smile.

"I'm Claire," she said, in a polished, privately educated voice. "I suppose you might say I'm your superintendent, care officer, concierge, and private nurse all in one." Her eyes sparkled at "private nurse" and he wondered if she was consciously flirting. If she even knew she was doing it.

Let's find out.

"Were you the one who changed my underwear?"

"Ah, now that would be telling," she grinned, and he decided that she knew she was flirting. She was accustomed to being desired, and reveled in it.

She placed her briefcase on the coffee table and stood with her hands on her hips. "You've worked out that we have you under surveillance, then?" she said.

"Yes. Why do you need to do that?"

"Don't they tell you these things?" she said, with mock irritation. "They really should, you know. You're the prize in a high-stakes game and your identity is closely guarded, your whereabouts a secret. The only thing our players know about you is that you're a Royal Marine commando. Thus we have to make sure you're kept free from any interference or communication. We don't want to give any of the players an advantage now, do we?"

"It's a competition?" asked Shelley.

"Bloody hell, I'm going to have to have a word with Tremain—he really didn't tell you anything, did he? Yes, of course it's a competition, with quite a purse for the winner. Mr. Miyake is the current holder, but there's a few who will be hoping to claim his title."

"Where does all this take place? Here?"

"No, in the woods somewhere. I trust you're an outdoorsman?"

"You have to be, in the Marines."

"You should be in your element, then."

Shelley pulled at his overalls. "Where are my clothes?"

"We're having them fumigated. You can have them back when the game is over, if you like. I mean, if you insist."

"Yes, I do insist," he said. "I'd like my clothes back."

"You'll be able to afford some new ones when this is all over."

He looked at her, seeing through her facade, seeing how much she was enjoying herself, and then forced himself to grin. "Yeah, of course. Old habits."

She returned his smile. "And you play in the overalls, of course."

"Am I supposed to look like a prisoner?"

"It's not intentional."

"So I'm not a prisoner here, then? I can come and go as I want?"

She furrowed her brow. "Well, no, of course you can't. There are all those pesky security issues I was talking about. But first you might want to know where 'here' is. Can't go into geographical detail, I'm afraid, but it's an old reformatory school. These buildings were the staff dwellings. There's a main school building and there are education blocks. There is also a gym, a swimming pool, a cinema, and a library. Most of the complex is abandoned, but what bits you need are fully kitted out for your exclusive use. You are invited—one might almost say 'required'—to use the swimming pool and gym on a daily basis. Use the cinema and library as you like, but we do insist that you maintain an exercise routine, eat well, and abstain from alcohol and drugs, which is just as well, because of course there will be no drink or drugs available."

"And I'm forbidden to leave the complex?"

She laughed. "'Fraid so."

"What if I change my mind and don't want to be a part of it anymore?"

"We hope that won't occur."

"But what if it does?"

"Then we'll cross that bridge when we come to it. Now," she said, changing the subject, "it's time for your medical. I'm going to need a urine sample and your fingerprint, for programming internal security."

"My fingerprint?"

"Yes, we need it for internal security," smiled Claire. "I'll also be taking blood, but before we start..." She wrinkled her nose. "How about I give you half an hour to take a shower?"

She left and he watched her go, his mind on what he knew about hostage situations. Be courteous with your captors, but remember that any warmth they show you is purely procedural. Don't let them get too close and, above all, whatever you do, don't get too close to them.

Why? Because at some point you might have to kill them.

CHAPTER 18

IN A DIMLY lit room in the bowels of a private members' club in Soho, the key members of The Quarry Company were meeting: the company's head of security, Tremain, and the two owners, Curtis and Boyd.

Curtis and Boyd liked to refer to themselves as "administrators," since there was nothing of The Quarry Company to own, not in the conventional sense. What they had was more precious than bricks and mortar, brand-name recognition, copyrights, trademarks, or patents. They had information. And information, as they and their clients knew, was power.

They were both in their early forties and wore jeans, polo shirts, and sweaters. If it looked as though life had been good to them, then that's because it had. They were both the recipients of expensive educations and favors that had sped them up the career ladder in multinational investment banks.

With such an effortless ascent came boredom, and the two Chelsea housemates compensated the usual way: hookers, drugs, and watching videos on YouTube in the down time between hookers and drugs.

One night they were watching videos of homeless men being paid by filmmakers to fight. Not long after that, Boyd and Curtis staged their own "bumfights" for their friends, and what they quickly noticed was that their friends rarely talked of them, and even then only in the most guarded terms. Other illicit activities were fair game for a good laugh in the pub, but not the bumfights.

One of the participants was killed, and for months Curtis and Boyd were terrified the death would be investigated. As it turned out, neither of them needed to work their contacts in the police force; there was no investigation. And that gave them the idea for The Quarry Company.

The rest, as they say, is history. It turned out that the omertà they'd noticed in their days organizing bumfights was multiplied a hundredfold when it came to the activities of The Quarry Company. They soon had a respectable client base who knew the rules; who even saw the activities of The QC as an act of insurrection against the political-correctness lobby, the do-gooders.

Whatever their reasons, whatever inspired them, the clients looked to The QC to provide them with something the outside world could not. And Curtis and Boyd were happy to provide it.

Over the course of three hunts, so far they had made

around £120 million profit, but more importantly they had accrued undreamed-of influence. It was no exaggeration to say that they had the Establishment in their pocket, and as far as Curtis and Boyd were concerned, there was no reason it shouldn't stay there.

"How is the quarry?" asked Curtis.

Tremain replied, "Claire reports excellent progress. He's adapting well to life at reform school."

"Good. Will he be ready for this weekend?"

"Oh, he was ready before we met him; according to Claire, he's an excellent physical specimen."

"Good. Well done. Pleased to hear it."

Boyd leaned forward to where his briefcase rested on a low table. He opened it, momentarily fiddled with the laptop inside, then closed it again.

"I hope you don't keep details of hunts on that thing," said Tremain.

"The bare minimum, and it's all encrypted," replied Boyd. "Our main archive is in a safe deposit box."

"That where your bodies are buried, is it?"

"It's biometrically protected. Basically you need to be me or Boyd to see it. Everything else is up here." Curtis tapped the side of his head. "Why do you ask? What's the interest?"

"You have to be able to drop everything and walk away, if need be. Nothing incriminating. No paper trail."

"Of course. But why bring that up now?"

"Well, it could be something, could be nothing, but we have an issue." The two men looked sharply at him, so Tremain kept it simple. "It's information from Kenneth Farmer. Sarah has become suspicious and she's been talking to a third party."

Curtis made a disgusted sound. "That idiot, Farmer. What kind of third party?"

"She corresponds with a 'Simon,' initials 'SC.' It would seem likely that this is Simon Claridge, an MI5 operative. They had a relationship at Cambridge and have remained close ever since."

"You know this man Claridge?"

"He's in another section, different floor. I see him in the lift occasionally. He's younger but older, if you know what I mean. He has a decent rank and a reputation as a good man. If he does suspect anything, then he's too clever to go making a song and dance about it. What we need to know is if he can link Farmer to anyone else in the organization. You two, for instance. Have you ever met Farmer?"

"We did, once," admitted Curtis.

Tremain grimaced and rubbed the back of his neck. "That was a little reckless, if I may say so."

Curtis shrugged. "Kenneth Farmer is one of those who offers us favors, in order to supplement his fee. Occasionally we have to meet him to discuss this. Besides, you taught us well, Obi Wan. We made sure of using the CCTV dead zones."

"Well, if you'd been identified, your names would have come up on the grid and I'd have been alerted. So let's assume, for the time being, that Claridge hasn't made the connection. In that case, he's a man with a suspicion, and not much else."

"He'll start digging," whined Boyd. "This is just the start of the investigation. Farmer's playing this weekend. This man Claridge could follow him to the hunt. Look, this is all getting too hot for me. Oakleigh's death, and now this. We should call it off."

Curtis sighed. "We have over seventy million riding on this hunt—we're not going to call it off. If there's a leak, we plug it."

"You're both right," said Tremain. "We need to neutralize the threat ahead of this weekend or we will have to cancel."

"We're not canceling," insisted Curtis. "It's your job to sort it, so sort it."

"Yes. For fuck's sake, Tremain," blurted Boyd, sweat glistening on his forehead, "do what you're paid for. Kill Claridge. Make it look like an accident. We can't afford any leaks."

Tremain looked at the two of them, trying to keep the distaste off his face. "Look, don't panic, either of you. We need to take Claridge out of the equation, but the last thing we want to do is raise Sarah Farmer's suspicions. The obvious course of action is to bring Claridge on board."

Tremain did his best to calm the two bankers, but even so, he was beginning to form suspicions of his own. What he heard from the reformatory was ringing alarm bells. He'd be making some investigations of his own before confronting Claridge.

"And if he doesn't want to come on board?" said Curtis. "You said he was a good man. What if he just wants to bring us down?"

Tremain smiled. "Claridge has a family. We'll be sure to use the carrot *and* the stick."

CHAPTER 19

SHELLEY STAVED OFF the boredom of his days at the reformatory school with exercise, Bruce Willis movies, and paperback novels.

He was virtually alone. The guards he saw kept their distance, restricting contact to a cheery wave. Surveillance was conducted via CCTV cameras. Shelley occupied himself with trying to spot them all.

Forming the perimeter was a sturdy partition wall. From the outside it would look like just another long-germinating suburban development, and even if you managed to bypass the CCTV and security guards to get inside, you wouldn't see much. Most of it was as Claire had described, a vision in rack and ruin. The walkways and service roads were cracked and strewn with weeds and litter; the buildings were rundown, almost every window smashed.

All, that was, apart from the area he considered to be his living quarters—the apartment, gym, swimming pool— which were disguised behind doors that looked ramshackle, but were in fact reinforced with steel bolts. The locks were operated using discreet fingerprint security, and he never quite got over the sense of passing through a portal, from an old derelict world into something modern and gleaming.

All of the doors he'd tried accepted his fingerprint, apart from one: the main gate, wide enough to allow for vehicles. He'd located the scanner and tried his index finger, but the gate stayed shut. Through a gap he could see a portable building that he took to be a guardhouse, and he pictured Claire inside watching him, enjoying the show. He half expected her to make an appearance, gently chiding him for his attempts to leave.

At night the complex was lit and he was able to use it just as he could during the day, but he made sure to get his rest, sleeping at night. The daytime was spent preparing. Mentally, mainly, but also physically. When he was in the swimming pool and his hands were invisible to the CCTV cameras, he massaged them, working his double-jointed thumbs. If he was right, then slipping out of handcuffs would prove to be essential.

"Hello, Captain Hodge," Claire said when she came at midday.

"It's Hodges," he corrected her.

"Oh, I am sorry. And here was me, trying to find out how you're getting on."

"Haven't you been watching me?"

"Watching you tells me what you're doing. It doesn't tell me how you're getting on."

"Well, I'm getting on fine, thank you very much. How much longer will I be here?"

"I'm afraid I can't tell you that," she smiled.

He had to admit, it was disarming, that smile. The kind of smile that took your mind off what you'd asked in the first place.

"Do you know?" he asked.

"I do. But I can't tell you."

"Why is that?"

"Security. Questions, questions…"

"You're the first person I've spoken to in two days, of course I'm going to have questions. When do I get my money?"

"On completion of the job. In the meantime, you do know you're being very well looked after, don't you?"

"All this, just for a game?"

"It's much more than just a game," she said, as though parroting a manual. "What we offer is a bespoke service. We offer excellence. Or at least the *illusion* of excellence. Which is why you need to be in good condition. Your medical has been a total success. The best I've ever had, in fact. No alcohol in you, which is very unusual. No drugs, either. You must be the most abstemious homeless man there ever was."

"I'm pleased to hear it."

"How did you end up on the streets?" she asked, settling into the sofa.

He told her a well-rehearsed story, one that corresponded with the details on Captain Steve Hodges's file, and she listened intently, nodding, smiling sympathetically. Every inch the confidante.

When he'd finished, her smile remained, but instead of following up with more questions or changing the subject, her eyes stayed fixed on his. "Can I ask you a question, Captain Hodges?" she said. Her voice had dropped. It was a little more husky.

"You can," he said, cautiously.

"Why haven't you made a pass at me? Every other contestant we've had here has tried his luck, but not you. Most of them…" she waved a hand as though put off by the idea. "But you're the first one I might have considered."

"What can I say? I'm a perfect gentleman. That and…" He pointed upwards, indicating the camera.

For a moment he thought she was about to put a move on him, and he steeled himself to resist. He'd always had a soft spot for borderline-sadistic girls, especially when they wore it as well as Claire did.

But she stood, seemingly satisfied. "I'll see you in a few days, Captain Hodges. Keep up the good work. I'll need to appraise you for my employers, and at the moment you can be sure it'll be a glowing report."

With Claire gone, Shelley sat and thought. He was being tested, no doubt about it. Were they suspicious? For the first time he wondered about the wisdom of staying clean. It marked him out, and not in a good way.

He found himself chewing his lip, wondering what they knew and what they were planning. If his cover were blown, they'd have confronted him by now. He'd be food for pigs.

Wouldn't he?

CHAPTER 20

CLARIDGE HAD FINISHED watching CCTV film taken from outside the Ten Bells pub on Commercial Street. The only relevant footage was a brief glimpse of the back of a tan jacket as its wearer disappeared into the pub. Like the two men who had met Kenneth Farmer, this one had known to use CCTV dead spots.

Just then came a knock at the frosted glass of his office door, and he looked up to see a figure outside—a figure wearing a tan leather jacket.

Claridge closed the viewing application on his computer and went to the door. There stood Hugh Tremain of D Section, wearing the selfsame jacket Claridge had just seen on the CCTV footage. Tremain carried a laptop. "Might I have a word, Simon?" he smiled.

Claridge swallowed, trying not to let his apprehension show. "Of course. You mind if I leave the door open while we talk? It's getting a bit stuffy in here."

"I'd prefer that you didn't. It's a rather...sensitive matter."

It was past seven in the evening, and the open-plan office behind them was almost empty. "We've more or less got the place to ourselves," said Claridge, and with a meaningful look at Tremain added, "I'll leave it open, if you don't mind."

"Sure, whatever you say. Your office."

Claridge hurried back to his desk.

"What did I interrupt?" asked Tremain, placing his laptop on Claridge's desk and sitting.

"Oh, nothing too important." Claridge glanced nervously at Tremain's laptop as his fingers danced on the keyboard.

"So what are you typing then?" asked Tremain pleasantly. He sat back and crossed his legs.

"It's procedure to log visitors."

"Yes, of course. I usually do mine when my visitor has departed."

Claridge continued to type, then pressed return.

"All done?" smiled Tremain.

"All done," Claridge smiled back.

"No point in trying to kill you now, then?"

Claridge didn't even blink. Didn't give Tremain the satisfaction. "Is that your intention, is it? To kill me?"

Tremain chuckled. "If it was, would I do it here in the office, do you think?"

"Your organization seems to favor hiding in plain sight."

"Does it? Really? Is that so?"

The two men fell silent and Claridge was glad of a moment to gather his thoughts. He'd been exposed somehow. But how? And how much did they know? And what the bloody hell was Tremain doing in his office?

"I won't insult your intelligence by asking you how much you know about us," Tremain was saying. He slouched, but watched Claridge carefully. "You'd be a fool to tell me. The point is you know *something,* and that's enough to worry my associates. As you're well aware, we're in the business of containing information, Simon. We nurture it, protect it. We take care it doesn't go anywhere it shouldn't. But when it does—well, then we need to do something about it."

"Are you talking as an MI5 man or in some other capacity?" asked Claridge, probing gently.

"Bit of both. The lines are blurred."

"So—what? You plan to buy my silence?"

"Well, that depends. Can your silence be bought?"

Claridge made a small scoffing sound. "What you're involved with is inhuman. It's despicable."

"That's a no, is it?"

"You bet your life it's a no. You need to be stopped."

"I see. And you're the man to do it, are you? Simon Claridge in the giddy heights of F Section is going to bring us down?"

Claridge felt himself deflate a little.

"No, I thought not," smiled the other man. "Problem is, you've been rumbled, and that makes you less than useless. There's not a thing you can do now."

"I should be silenced then. What are you waiting for?"

Tremain sighed. "Look, wet work is by definition messy. But even more than that, we don't *want* to terminate you, Simon; we'd rather have you as an asset. We want to bring you into the fold. You accept our money, you become implicated—we're all happy."

Claridge shook his head. "I can't sit by and let you continue. I can't. I couldn't live with myself."

Tremain rolled his eyes, but the gesture was too theatrical to convince Claridge. *He's got something up his sleeve,* he thought. *Something to do with that laptop.* "Oh, come on. Don't make this difficult, for God's sake. Take the money, tell me what I want to know, and we can tie off this whole sorry business and look forward to a future of giving each other little knowing winks in the lift."

"What do you mean? What do you want to know?"

Tremain leaned forward. He put one hand on Claridge's desk, close to the laptop.

"I'll be honest. I was telling a fib when I said I wasn't going to ask you what you knew. In fact, I want to know exactly what you know."

"Very little, is the answer," replied Claridge cautiously.

"Okay. Enough pretending. I know that's not the case. I know because I checked. I checked your requisitions. CCTV of Chancery Lane, close to a lawyer's office. That was interesting. But perhaps even more revealing than that was the CCTV of Commercial Street that you asked to review, close to a certain pub I frequent." Tremain paused to pin Claridge with a look. "You were looking for me, weren't you?"

A pause.

"Yeah, I know you were. So of course I had to ask myself *why* you were looking for me. Why me? Why there? So I studied the same CCTV, and guess what I saw?"

"Go on…"

"I saw Captain Steve Hodges paying a great deal of attention to what was going on inside the pub. Which led me to the conclusion that it was Captain Steve Hodges who tipped you off about me. I think it was, wasn't it? I think you've got a man on the inside, and it's him."

Claridge felt his palms sweat, but he tried to bluff it out. "I wish I did. This conversation might make sense. But I'm afraid your thinking isn't as joined-up as you'd like to believe. I don't know any Captain Steve Hodges."

"No, of course you don't. Captain Hodges is dead. I'm surprised you didn't ascertain that on your visits to Records. Obviously you didn't log the real reason as your 'purpose for visit,' but it's not too difficult to pull the wool over old Sparkles's eyes, is it? I'm guessing you were there to doctor Hodges's records in order that your man on the inside could plausibly assume his identity. Am I right?"

Claridge felt himself go cold. Dread rose inside him.

"I need to know the *real* identity of your man. I need to know now."

"You can go fuck yourself," replied Claridge.

"I thought you might say that. Which is why…"

Tremain reached to open the laptop.

CHAPTER 21

THERE WAS A handful of staff still working in the open-plan area outside Claridge's office, but none could see what was on the laptop screen. The two images that greeted Claridge were for his eyes only.

Tremain had sized two windows so that both views were visible. The image on the left showed the outside of Claridge's house. His front-room curtains were open and his wife and younger daughter were playing Scrabble inside. Everything about the scene was normal and serene—apart from the fact that he was viewing it through a telescopic sight, complete with a duplex crosshair.

The image on the right was fuzzier, but more colorful. This one was taken from a phone placed on the table in a bar. It showed his elder daughter and her friend. They'd gone out together to celebrate the friend gaining a place at university, but they'd been joined by two older men who were trying to chat them up. Or at least that's what they were pretending to do. The phone transmitting the footage belonged to one of the men.

The two girls were laughing politely at the attempts of the two men to impress them, but Claridge knew his daughter. He saw the signs. He knew full well that later on she'd be telling him about the sleazy guys who spoiled their evening.

If there was a later.

"One phone call and the guy on the left pulls the trigger," said Tremain flatly. "A second call and the two guys on the right show your daughter what they've learned from watching porn. And do you know how long it took me to set that up, my friend? Less than five minutes. *That* is how easy it is to crush you."

"I'll kill you for this," said Claridge, without much conviction.

"No, you won't. Remember what I said. You're in the open now, no cards to play. You should be grateful you're not being followed home by a man with a syringe. You should be grateful you even have the choice. Do as you're told and you could come out of this rich, and with peace of mind that your family is safe. Now, tell me the name of your operative. And bear in mind, I'm not leaving here until I've verified his identity. Say it—say his name."

"I'd be signing his death warrant."

"Either way, you're signing someone's death warrant." Tremain looked almost regretful. "Look, we're not playing here, Simon."

Claridge shook his head with disgust. "What happened to you? What happened to make you like this?"

"I've asked myself the same question," replied Tremain. "I asked myself: did I really get involved with MI5 to help the rich and powerful kill the downtrodden? And I decided that the answer is that I had no choice. It will happen regardless. I might as well make hay while the sun shines. Now give me the name, before I make some calls."

Claridge's eyes dropped and he spoke Shelley's name into his lap.

In a moment Tremain had a home address and men were dispatched.

Together they waited for further updates, their eyes on Tremain's laptop screen.

CHAPTER 22

LUCY WASN'T NORMALLY so diligent when it came to checking her emails, but with Shelley away, she'd been spending more time online. Facebook, eBay, Etsy, you name it.

It was for this reason that she saw Claridge's message as soon as it was sent: *We're blown. Expect enemy action ASAP.*

She ran upstairs and retrieved a Glock 17 sidearm from the cupboard. At the same time she grabbed a framed photograph from a chest of drawers, and then on her return downstairs snatched a second picture from the wall. She rearranged the remaining pictures to hide the gap.

Now, in the front room, she tried to view their house as visitors might see it, looking for anything incriminating. Satisfied, she stashed the Glock and the two pictures on a shelf inside the chimney, away from all but the most thorough search.

Right, she thought. She was as ready as she could be, in the time allowed. She warmed up as she waited.

Shortly afterwards a minivan drew up outside. Four men

alighted and two moved off. Probably going to the back of the house.

She drew away from the window as the other two approached her front door and knocked. Frankie padded through from the kitchen as she went to answer.

In Claridge's office at Thames House, Tremain was on the phone. "Visual ID. You think it's him? Okay. That's the wife. Name of Lucy. Find something that belongs to him, run a fingerprint check, and get back to me."

He ended the call and looked across to where Claridge sat with rounded shoulders. "It checks out so far. Captain David Shelley of the SAS. Exemplary record. My compliments, Claridge, you've certainly given us cause for concern."

His phone rang again.

"Hello. It checks out? Good. Get out of there. You know what to do."

He listened.

"Fine," he said. "Use a suppressor."

PART THREE

CHAPTER 23

"YOU'LL NEED TO sleep in your overalls tonight," Claire had told him.

He'd looked sharply at her. "It's happening tomorrow, then? Saturday?"

"Your weekend starts here," she'd said brightly.

Sure enough, Shelley awoke with a knee in his chest and arms pinning his legs. Before he could move, his wrists were cuffed with a strange-looking pair of handcuffs.

He stood and Claire led him out of the bedroom and into the living area. Two of the security men busied themselves putting on his boots.

"What are these?" he asked Claire, raising his hands.

"Cool, aren't they? Electronic handcuffs. You might say they have an interesting unlocking mechanism."

Surreptitiously he moved his hands inside the bracelets. Thank God they weren't done up too tight. These he could negotiate.

"Why do you need them?"

"I'm sorry," she said cheerfully, "it's just procedure—nothing personal. You'll be handcuffed until the hunt begins."

"Are you going to be the one doing the un-handcuffing?"

"'Fraid not. You'll be on your own in the woods by then. The handcuffs will be detonated. That's the interesting unlocking mechanism I was talking about. *Kerboom!* When it happens, try to keep your hands as far from the center of the cuffs as possible."

"Will it hurt?"

She pulled a face. "The explosion is mostly internal, but yes, it will hurt a little."

They formed a procession to a waiting minivan with blacked-out windows. *Handcuffs, but no blindfold,* thought Shelley as he settled in with Claire beside him, security men taking the other seats.

"So what happens now?" he asked.

"You sit back and enjoy the ride." She looked at her watch. "We'll be there in approximately two hours."

"And where's *there?*"

"Questions, questions. A country estate hired by The Quarry Company is the answer, home for the weekend. Things will be getting a little wild."

"And I'm the main attraction?"

She arched an eyebrow. "Don't get ideas above your station. You're *one* of the attractions. But there can be no hunt celebrations without a hunt to celebrate. So you are indeed crucial to the weekend's entertainment."

"Sounds interesting."

"Oh, things are about to get *very* interesting."

Two hours later they came to a set of ornate gates guarded by two men in black combat trousers and bomber jackets. The sentries carried HK MP5 submachine guns and wore comms devices at their throats, though one of them relayed the arrival of the minivan using a walkie-talkie, while the other one conducted a TSCM bug-sweep of the vehicle, greeting Claire by name.

Then they were allowed through, taking a long approach road up an incline to the grounds, where beautifully manicured lawns swept down to a treeline. As they climbed, Shelley's gaze went to what looked like miles and miles of woodland.

The kill zone.

On the front lawn of the stately home was the whole circus. A Hughes 500 personnel helicopter sat on the grass with its rotors drooping. Not far away stood a huge operations van, staffed by techs wearing headphones.

Meanwhile, the players stood in groups, attended to by butlers in black suits offering sherry, champagne, and nibbles. Some were dressed in traditional country tweed, the Savile Row country-gent look, and others in ostentatious combat garb, as though attending a military fancy-dress party. Shelley even saw one man smearing camouflage stick on his face.

All for little old me, he thought, and did a headcount. Twenty-five. They would have to be divided into squads, deployed in some kind of grid formation to minimize the risk of shooting each other.

Also there were clusters of security men, like the ones at the gate. *Christ!* He counted thirty. He hadn't expected that, but it made sense. Each player would have his own personal bodyguard. After all, The Quarry Company wouldn't want any harm coming to their players. Not after Lord Oakleigh. It was like Claire said: they wanted to provide risk but, more importantly, the illusion of risk.

There was something missing from the scene.

"Where are all the guns?" he asked Claire, as their transport reached the end of the approach road.

"Not sure," she said airily. "Maybe they haven't distributed them yet."

Their arrival had caused a ripple of interest to run through the men on the lawn. One by one, they turned to look at the car as it reached a gravel parking area and came to a halt.

"I love this bit," grinned Claire.

Shelley soon found out why, as with everybody on the lawn now looking at the car, she stepped out to be greeted by a raucous cheer. She milked it, calling, "I still have to

get dressed yet," provoking an even more boisterous greeting. "More girls arriving later," she winked, and the cheering
reached fever pitch.

She waited for it to die down, then gestured to Shelley,
who stepped out of the minivan with his arms handcuffed
before him like a convict. The men on the lawn hushed, as
though suddenly respectful. At the same time they were approached by three men: one was Tremain, who wore what
looked like a SIG Mosquito in a shoulder holster, under
his usual tan leather jacket. The other two were the same
pair who had met Kenneth Farmer at the lawyer's office on
Chancery Lane.

They thanked Claire and she gave them kisses in return,
reserving a more intimate kiss for Tremain, before trotting
off in the direction of the house. Now he stood with Tremain
and the two Quarry Company bosses, one of whom carried
a briefcase.

"I'm Mr. Curtis," said the other one, with a smile that
didn't reach his eyes. "This is Mr. Boyd." They all shook
hands. "You're familiar with the rules of the game?"

"Go over them again, if you would," asked Shelley.

Curtis pursed his lips. "It's simple. You'll be taken by Land
Rover to a spot in the woods, a secret spot known only to Mr.
Tremain. You see our operations van over there? From there
we'll detonate the cuffs. I trust Claire has told you all about
our ingenious exploding handcuffs?"

Shelley nodded.

"It'll hurt. I'm sorry about that." His wonky smile indicated that nothing could be further from the truth. "But it's a minor burn. I'm sure you'll consider it worth it."

"And on that subject, where's my money?"

"Oh, of course. Money." He pointed to Boyd's suitcase. "In there are two envelopes. The first is for ten thousand pounds. You get that whatever happens. There's also another ten thousand pounds, if you're able to reach the perimeter. You won't be getting that, though."

"Oh yes? Why's that?"

"Because you won't be winning. If you manage to evade us for too long, we deploy drones to look for you. Callous as it may seem, we—like our clients—like to win."

"By stacking the odds in their favor?"

"Now he gets it."

"And they're stopping me with paintball guns?"

"Something like that."

"Where are they, these guns? I'd be interested to see them."

Curtis wore a strained smile. "Not something you need to worry about. Now, why don't we go over and meet the players?"

They turned to depart from the parking area. At the same time an extraordinary thing took place on the lawn: the players arranged themselves into a line, like subjects about to meet the Queen. Some even removed their hats. For a moment, Shelley really did think he might be led along the line in order to shake each one by the hand. Instead, Curtis, Boyd, and Tremain took him to stand in front of the men.

"Quarry, show your handcuffs, please," ordered Curtis, and Shelley did as he was asked, trying to keep the contempt off his face. His eyes raked the line of men who stared at him with naked fascination. Among them was Kenneth Farmer, as well as a government minister he recognized. There was a Japanese man who wore a strange, enigmatic smile. *Was he the current holder of the title Claire had mentioned? Was he the one who killed Cookie?*

At his side, Curtis spoke again. "Gentlemen, we promised you a surprise, and a surprise you shall have. Please allow me to introduce the quarry by name."

He paused, and Shelley realized that the attention on him had intensified.

"You expected a Marine commando," said Curtis, building the expectation, "but we have something even more elite than that. An SAS captain: Captain David Shelley."

Tremain was looming over him. "Captain David Shelley, who—according to his military record—is double-jointed," he whispered, and snapped Shelley's handcuffs so tightly that they dug into his wrist.

Oh God, thought Shelley.

CHAPTER 24

THE PLAYERS WHOOPED and cheered. Shelley saw the grinning, triumphant faces of Curtis and Boyd, as Tremain and a trio of guards marched him towards a waiting Land Rover. The last thing he heard as he was bundled inside was a loudspeaker announcement: "Weapons distribution due in T minus five minutes," and then they were drawing away, leaving the lawn behind.

They drove, taking a route parallel to the treeline, and then took a left onto a service road that bisected the woodland area. Shelley's mind worked overtime. If his cover was blown, then maybe they'd got to Claridge and…

No, not Lucy. Please not Lucy.

"How did you find out?" he asked Tremain, injecting the right note of defeat into his voice.

Tremain had angled himself into the door so that he looked across the seat at Shelley, one hand close to his jacket, ready to draw his SIG. "You see Kenneth Farmer back there? He overheard his wife on the phone. From there, it was just a case of working out which man named Simon she was friendly with. Turned out to be my MI5 colleague, and your friend, Simon Claridge. He told us all we needed to know."

"You tortured it out of him?"

"We didn't need to," smiled Tremain.

He said no more, leaving Shelley to wonder if Claridge really had given him up in exchange for a bribe. *Had he given them Lucy, too?*

They drove on in silence for some moments. Shelley half expected the car to stop and the man in the passenger seat to turn around, a gun in his hand. Game over.

"So what happens now?" Shelley asked at last.

"Well, this is the funny thing," said Tremain as he gazed out of the window. "The hunt is to continue as normal. Your exposure as an infiltrator has made absolutely no difference at all. The company wants to put on a show. You're the show."

He's lying, thought Shelley. *Or maybe not lying—but he has something up his sleeve.*

They drew to a halt and the driver killed the engine. On both sides of the track, shallow channels gave way to thick woodland beyond, dark and forbidding despite the early morning light.

"Here we are then, Shelley," said Tremain. "Journey's end."

He got out and drew his gun. It was indeed a SIG, noted

Shelley. A SIG Mosquito, compact and light, but a small-caliber weapon with limited penetration and stopping power.

Tremain leveled it at Shelley. "Out," he said, and Shelley did as he was told, stepping into the uncanny quiet of the deserted woodland road, thinking this might be it. Ready to make his move, if Tremain's finger tightened on the trigger. "Let's go," said Tremain, and motioned towards the trees on the right.

Shelley relaxed a little. Tremain intended to kill him. He had no doubt. But not just yet.

The two in the front stayed with the car. The third guard reached for a short-bladed kukri knife from the map pocket, presumably for dealing with vegetation. Holstered at his leg was a Glock sidearm, and he carried an MP5. Now Shelley noticed something else about the weapons that made his heart sink. They were smart-protected, inset with sensors that responded to the user's palm print. Any hopes he had of grabbing one and using it were dashed.

"We're making our way into the kill zone," said Tremain into his walkie-talkie.

"Keep us informed," came the reply. "Weapons are distributed."

Shelley was directed into the treeline. Ahead of him went the guard, with Tremain bringing up the rear. Shelley's mind was working. He had to assume Tremain was planning to put a bullet in him, one in the back of the head perhaps, but he wouldn't want a gunshot being heard; he'd use a suppressor, and he hadn't fitted one yet.

Shelley needed to try to control this, stay on top of it. He sped up almost imperceptibly, coming closer to the guard in front.

"You know, you're making a mistake keeping me in the game," he said over his shoulder.

Tremain chuckled. "Wouldn't you know it? That's just what I told Curtis and Boyd. I told them that even once you were robbed of your advantage, you were still a threat. But, of course, men like that don't listen to men like me. They insisted the hunt go ahead, despite the danger."

"Then they're fools."

"You might say that. I couldn't possibly comment."

That's it, thought Shelley. A management disagreement. Curtis and Boyd thought the game should go on, but Tremain was more cautious than that; he was going to take care of Shelley, whether they liked it or not.

"But you're a cut above those two turkeys," Shelley called back, stealing a glance at the same time. Tremain still held the SIG, but one hand was in his jacket pocket. Reaching for the suppressor, perhaps.

"I like to think so," said Tremain.

"I think you'd be tempted to disobey that order, if you thought it was for the greater good."

He sped up a little more. The man on point was in range. Shelley was ready. He had to time this right.

"Disobey an order? Me?" Tremain was saying, but some instinct told Shelley that the moment had come, and he glanced behind in time to see Tremain fitting a suppressor to the SIG.

Now! Shelley hurtled forward, raised his handcuffed hands and looped them over the head of the guard, grabbing him in a choke hold and delivering a head butt to the back of the head at the same time.

The guard went limp in his arms as he swung him around to face Tremain. The MI5 man had fitted the suppressor and he raised the SIG two-handed, but bared his teeth in frustration when he saw that his shot was blocked. He pulled the trigger anyway. There was a soft *thunk* and the security guard shook as a round made a hole in his shoulder, but didn't make its way out the other side. *Thank God for the small caliber,* thought Shelley. But he wasn't waiting for Tremain to take another shot, and he dragged the security guy behind a tree.

Tremain ran to one side and there was a second *thunk* as he loosed off another round, this one striking the security guy in the stomach, instantly making his bomber jacket slick with blood.

With the guard dead by now, his feet dragged on the woodland floor as Shelley pulled him behind the cover of another tree trunk, hearing Tremain's running feet as the MI5 man tried to find a new line of fire. *Thunk!* A shot hit the tree in front of Shelley.

The guard was getting heavy and Shelley had no idea how long he could keep dodging Tremain. He needed to get close to him. The SIG carried ten rounds. If Tremain exhausted those, then maybe Shelley could rush him on the reload.

Peering over the shoulder of the security guard, he saw the MI5 man out in the open. *Thunk!* Shelley was showered with wood splinters.

"Out of practice, are you?" Shelley taunted. "When was the last time you shot at a target moving between cover? Do they teach you that in the civil service?"

He was thinking, *Come closer. Loose off a few more.*

But Tremain was ahead of him, and he reached for his walkie-talkie. "Quarry in position," he said. "Blow the cuffs. Repeat: blow the cuffs."

CHAPTER 25

THE CUFFS BLEW, making a hole in the security man's throat. Without the handcuffs to support his weight, Shelley felt the guard slipping out of his arms and Tremain took advantage of the increased target. *Thunk!* Shelley felt liquid warmth, but no pain, as a bullet grazed his shoulder. He crouched, grabbed the security man's hand and drew his sidearm, praying the guy's palm print would activate the Glock.

It did. Pressing the dead hand to the sensor, Shelley snatched his first shot and it went wild, but it was enough to put the fear of God into Tremain. The Quarry man returned fire. His bullets crashed into the foliage. Shelley fired two more his way, sending Tremain scurrying into cover. In the pause, Shelley cast his eye around, looking for the kukri.

In the distance Shelley heard the *parp*ing of a hunting bugle. The game had begun. At the same time Tremain's walkie-talkie was squawking. "What's going on? We heard gunfire."

"The quarry is loose and armed," Tremain replied, with panic in his voice. "Repeat: the quarry is loose and armed. Break all radio silence. Go to execution stage three at once."

And that was it for the Quarry's head of security. Evidently he'd decided that discretion was the better part of valor; he was making a dash for it. "Good luck, Shelley," he called. "You'll need it." Tremain ran, moving through the trees too fast for Shelley to get a bead on him.

Shelley found the kukri, and with two chops hacked off the security guy's hand. He held it up. He didn't need the fingers. He disposed of those too. A grisly job, but at least now he was able to operate the Glock and the MP5. He set off, moving stealthily, choosing a route that ran parallel to the access road but kept him in the trees. He heard the distant sound of drones approaching and grinned. Good to know he'd put them into emergency mode so quickly.

Then he stopped. There was an irregularity in the foliage ahead. His eyes adjusted and he saw the crouching man squinting through telescopic sights just in time to roll to one side as the shot crashed into the woods behind him.

At the same time, Shelley heard the crackle of a walkie-talkie. He swung his head to the left and saw a security man who would have had the drop on Shelley, if not for the walkie-talkie blowing his cover. Shelley swung the MP5 at the same time as the new arrival opened fire. They exchanged shots, neither with the luxury of time to aim. In the same moment the sniper tried a second shot, which came closer than the first. Shelley fired again at the guard, more accurately this time, raking a burst of bullets across his chest and seeing him spin away in a mist of blood. As the guard fell, he revealed the terrified husband of the Home Secretary crouching behind him, his hunting rifle at his shoulder. He fired but missed, and Shelley wasn't about to let him shoot a second time. A short burst from the MP5 and Kenneth Farmer jerked and fell.

A third sniper round tore into a tree above Shelley's head. He swung round and loosed two shots into the undergrowth in return, then crouched and took a more considered line of fire, spraying vegetation left to right, fast and high; then a second time, low.

He was rewarded with a scream.

For a moment there was silence as the woods settled in the aftermath of the gunfight. Then Shelley heard an urgent whispered voice. "Farmer and Miyake both down. Do you copy that? Farmer and Miyake down. Send everybody to my position. *Everybody*."

Shelley's MP5 used fifteen-round mags. He slammed another in, then squeezed off a burst to cover himself while changing position. Somewhere in the trees was a panicking security guard and what sounded like a wounded Miyake, but the drones were gathering overhead and he could hear more players and guards crashing through the undergrowth towards his position. All attempts at stealth—any pretense that this was a game—were now forgotten about.

"Hold your fire. Hold your fire until you have visual on me and Miyake," the security guard was gibbering. "Repeat, no indiscriminate fire."

He was waiting for reinforcements, but Shelley had his position now. Shelley came from behind his cover, found the target and neutralized it with a single shot. The guard fell, almost noiselessly.

Threat over, Shelley rose from cover. Not far away the wounded player was writhing, moaning with pain. Shelley moved over to him and saw that an MP5 round had made a mess of his upper thigh. "You're Mr. Miyake, are you?" he said.

He squinted down the gun sights at the man, who nodded. With his chin, Shelley indicated towards the Tracking-Point that lay on the ground.

"And you killed Cookie with that, did you?"

Miyake nodded. "He was a worthy opponent," he croaked. Whether that was supposed to comfort Shelley, he wasn't really sure.

Shelley's finger tightened on the trigger. Mr. Miyake saw and tensed. "Please," he said.

"You rich?" asked Shelley.

Mr. Miyake nodded his head furiously. "A billionaire," he said. "I'll give you anything."

"Good. Make it fifty million to homeless charities by Thursday. And if it's not done, I'll come for you and it'll cost you a lot more than fifty million, I can promise you that. Do you believe me?"

Miyake nodded.

"Good. You're right to."

And with that, Shelley took off.

A round crashed into the foliage around him. He fired a burst in return and heard the sound of the gunman beating a retreat. He stopped, checked the angle of sunlight coming through the trees, mentally recalibrated his position, and set off. This time he was going towards the access road. Now he had a plan.

He slowed as he reached the perimeter, then stopped, seeing a guard as well as a Land Rover parked on the road. There would be a sentry on the far side, guarding the treeline. The idea was to bottle Shelley in.

Right. It was crucial he did this without being spotted.

Shelley flitted through the undergrowth, moving from tree to tree in time with the guard's diligent scanning from left to right. Each move brought him closer and he was pleased that the buzzing of the drones canceled out what minimal sound he made. Gently he let the MP5 fall to its sling, crouching, ready to make his move.

The sound of drones increased suddenly, and Shelley looked up to see one above his position. He couldn't let it report his location, and with a curse he snatched up the MP5 and took it out. The two security guards were startled into action, and Shelley swung the barrel in an arc, putting two rounds in the man closest to him. The sentry on the far side dived behind the Land Rover and Shelley went down to his stomach, tucking the submachine gun into his shoulder and tracking the man in the space beneath the chassis. He fired. Once. Twice. The guy screamed and was still.

Shelley ran to the road and checked the bodies. He grabbed more magazines from them, as much ammo as he could carry. He smiled. Everything was going according to plan now.

With the road clear, he set off once more, storming upwards for about two hundred yards and then taking a sudden left into the treeline and back into the woods. He moved quickly but stealthily, hoping he'd timed this right....

He had. With their backs to him was a pair of hunters, a player and his security. They were joining a haphazard pincer movement that was trying to trap Shelley, but he'd anticipated them and now dropped quietly to one knee, finding the guard in the sights of his MP5.

He hated himself for doing it the coward's way, but he put two bullets in the guy's back. The player cursed in German and panicked, running off into the woods. Shelley fired after him, deliberately missing, but his shots had the intended effect. Other nervous players, unaware that their fellow competitors were being driven towards them, opened fire.

There was shouting, confusion, more shots fired, and more screams.

Good. It was just as Shelley had hoped. He fired off an entire magazine indiscriminately into the woods. Let them deal with that.

CHAPTER 26

"HE'S GOT THEM killing each other. It's pandemonium down there," said Tremain. He stood in the reception hall of the great home with the two other organizers, the crackle of gunfire reaching them through the open front door. Curtis and Boyd had been hoping things would somehow sort themselves out. Tremain's expression told them nothing could be further from the truth.

"We've got to evacuate," insisted the MI5 man. "This guy won't stop. He's got a job to do and he won't stop until it's done. I've seen him in action—he's a fucking machine. You have to know when to withdraw, gentlemen, and that time is now."

Boyd was dancing from foot to foot. "Come on, Curtis, let's go."

"We still have our security," said Curtis. Even so, he was checking his own weapon.

"Get her in here," said Tremain. "You're going to need her with you."

"She's our bargaining chip. He'll have to surrender," Curtis replied.

"For Christ's sake," snarled Tremain, "you're past the point where you can win this. All you can do is hope to get out alive. Go for the chopper. I'll take a Land Rover."

His walkie-talkie squawked. "Quarry spotted. He's coming your way."

"Well, stop him then!" snarled Tremain, but he knew threats and commands were useless now. If the security men had any sense, they'd be steering clear of Shelley. There were too many bodies and not enough accountability. There was no reason to die here. No reason at all.

"Claire, bring her through," called Curtis over his shoulder.

A door opened. Through it came Claire. She had changed and wore an evening gown, complete with a long slit to the thigh. She wore an expression of concern, something that didn't come easily to her. By her side, cuffed with cable ties, was Lucy.

"What's going on?" asked Claire.

"We're fucked, is what's going on," said Tremain.

Lucy's silence and calmness had been unnerving the Quarry men, but when she heard Tremain speak, she looked sharply at him. "You're the one on the phone," she said.

"So?" said Tremain.

"You gave the order to shoot Frankie."

"What's this, Tremain?" asked Curtis. Even in their moment of defeat he seemed intrigued.

"We had to shoot the dog," explained Tremain.

"He'll kill you for that, you know," said Lucy.

Tremain spoke into his walkie-talkie. "Start up. Curtis and Boyd are coming, plus the woman."

From outside the sound of the helicopter engine intensified.

"I'll be in touch," Tremain said to Curtis and Boyd, and then to Claire, "Let's go."

From outside came the clatter of gunfire.

Shelley was getting closer.

CHAPTER 27

IN THE REARVIEW mirror of the Land Rover he'd commandeered, Shelley saw chaos spilling from the treeline and onto the lawn, as security men and players came tumbling out of the woods, wide-eyed and terrified. He saw at least one pair of men carrying a body, and security guards screaming into walkie-talkies and comms devices. A Motorola unit he'd taken from one of the guards was alive with shrieks, screams for help, and appeals for calm.

But now he saw activity at the house. The rotors of the helicopter were in full spin and people were leaving in their droves. He saw men in butlers' uniforms piling into a minivan. Frantic techs were packing up the operations van. Land Rovers spat gravel as they hightailed it away from the parking area and hurtled down the approach road, as employees abandoned ship.

Amid the commotion, Shelley saw Tremain. The MI5 man and Claire were joining the evacuation, dashing across to a parked Land Rover. Shelley was about to alter course and stop them, when he saw the figures of Curtis and Boyd appear on the steps to the front door of the home. Curtis held a sidearm, Boyd held his suitcase. They were making their way to the chopper.

And with them was Lucy. All thoughts of taking Tremain evaporated as Shelley wrenched the wheel to the left, steering the Land Rover onto the lawn and aiming it towards the waiting helicopter.

Curtis and Boyd saw him. They looked from the helicopter to the Land Rover and Shelley saw them frozen in time. Curtis decided not to make the dash and hauled Lucy back; Boyd decided to chance it and increased his speed; the helicopter pilot was desperately unbuckling as the black Land Rover hurtled towards him.

Shelley threw up his hands to protect his face as the Land Rover plowed into Boyd, then crunched into the chopper. The banker screamed in pain, crushed between the car and the helicopter. Feeling blood ooze down his forehead, Shelley emptied half a magazine into the instrumentation in the cockpit and then finished off Boyd. The screaming stopped and the rotors were slowing as Shelley rolled out of the shattered Land Rover and landed on the lawn.

There was no time to recover. His shoulder and head shrieked with pain, but he was already under attack. A bullet slapped into the metal shell of the helicopter, and Shelley turned to see Curtis firing wildly. Using the buckled door of the Land Rover for cover, Shelley trained his sights on Curtis, about to take him down and finish the job.

But Curtis saw the danger. He scuttled behind Lucy, using her as a shield, the pistol at her temple.

The helicopter wound down, finally becoming silent. From the woods came the occasional rattle of gunfire and shouts of confusion. Otherwise, a curious silence had descended on the lawn.

"Throw down your weapon, Shelley, or I'll put a bullet in her," commanded Curtis.

"You'd probably miss," Shelley said calmly. He could just make out the tiniest sliver of Curtis behind Lucy. Couldn't risk a shot.

"It's all over," called Curtis. "We're going to make our way to a Land Rover, and if you love your wife, you won't try to stop us."

Shelley didn't blink. "Didn't she tell you about us?" he called.

"We haven't had time to become acquainted," sneered Curtis.

"It might have been a good idea. She could have told you what she did before marrying me."

"What are you talking about?"

"I'm talking about the three-man team in Afghanistan. It was me, Cookie, and a third operative. Only thing is, there weren't three *men* in our team. One of them was a woman."

It was the cue for Lucy to make her move. She sidestepped and elbowed Curtis at the same time, a move so fast it was almost blurred.

And it gave Shelley all the time he needed.

He fired once. Curtis grew a third eye in the center of his forehead and dropped.

CHAPTER 28

Four months later

TREMAIN ESCAPED THE midday Spanish heat and came inside from the pool area, and the first thing he saw was Claire lying facedown on the floor tiles.

She wore her bikini, and she was still breathing. In his final moments Tremain was grateful for the fact that she wasn't dead; that the revenge wasn't to be merciless and indiscriminate.

Because what Tremain knew at once was that Shelley had found him.

Sure enough, the next thing he saw was Shelley, sitting on his sofa with a suppressed pistol trained on him.

"Shelley," said Tremain, and Shelley shot him in the foot.

He hit the floor hard, and the random thought that he wished he wouldn't have to die wearing swimming trunks occurred to him.

Shelley stood up and walked over.

"Hello, Tremain," he said.

Tremain stared up at him, his mouth working, no words coming out.

"You didn't honestly think I'd let you get away with it, did you?" asked Shelley. He crouched. "I mean, I can accept that the Establishment managed to convince everyone that it was a terrorist attack at the estate; that the world at large believes Kenneth Farmer and Cowie and Kiehl and Curtis and Boyd all died heroes trying to stop it. And I might not even have minded that you and Claire escaped, because after all, there will always be more men like you, whose services are available to the highest bidder; and there will always be more women like Claire, who view other people as playthings for their own pleasure. What I do mind about, however, is my dog."

He straightened, looking down the barrel of his Glock at Tremain writhing on the blood-soaked tiles.

"This," he said, "this is for Frankie."

On the road they said their good-byes: Claridge going to his car, Lucy and Shelley going to theirs, all three satisfied that justice had been served.

"I heard about the City of London vault robbery," said Shelley. "Was that anything to do with you?"

"The one in which a safe deposit box belonging to Messrs. Curtis and Boyd was stolen?" smiled Claridge. "No, nothing to do with me at all."

"So what happens to all that incriminating information?" asked Lucy, sparkling and beautiful in the hot sun.

"It stays under lock and key," said Claridge.

"Until such time as it's needed?" asked Shelley wryly. "Quite some insurance policy you've amassed there."

"I didn't ask for it, Shelley," said Claridge.

Shelley nodded. Claridge was one of the good guys.

Claridge had asked before they left, "What will you do now?" At the time they'd given him noncommittal answers, but now, sitting in the car, Shelley and Lucy considered their options for real.

The plan had been to stage their own deaths. On the other side of a metal barrier was a cliff face, the sea below: *Couple Killed in Deadly Crash* was the plan. Bodies lost at sea.

But on the other hand, they wanted to live their lives, restart their company, be a normal couple.

They sat for more than two hours talking it over, until at last they reached a decision.

"Ready?" he said.

"Ready," she replied.

He threw the car into gear and floored the accelerator.

ABOUT THE AUTHORS

JAMES PATTERSON has written more bestsellers and created more enduring fictional characters than any other novelist writing today. He lives in Florida with his family.

ANDREW HOLMES's first novel, *SLEB*, was shortlisted for the 2002 W.H. Smith New Talent Award in the U.K. He lives in the English countryside with his wife and two children.

"ALEX CROSS, I'M COMING FOR YOU...."

Gary Soneji, the killer from *Along Came a Spider,* has been dead for more than ten years—but Cross swears he saw Soneji gun down his partner. Is Cross's worst enemy back from the grave?

Nothing will prepare you for the wicked truth.

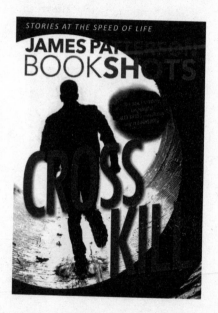

Read the next riveting, pulse-racing Alex Cross adventure, available now only from

BOOK**SHOTS**

MICHAEL BENNETT FACES HIS TOUGHEST CASE YET....

Detective Michael Bennett is called to the scene after a man plunges to his death outside a trendy Manhattan hotel—but the man's fingerprints are traced to a pilot who was killed in Iraq years ago.

Will Bennett discover the truth?

Or will he become tangled in a web of government secrets?

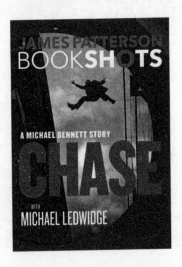

Read the new action-packed Michael Bennett story,
Chase, **available now only from**

BOOKSHOTS

"I'M NOT ON TRIAL. SAN FRANCISCO IS."

Drug cartel boss the Kingfisher has a reputation for being violent and merciless. And after he's finally caught, he's set to stand trial for his vicious crimes—until he begins unleashing chaos and terror upon the lawyers, jurors, and police associated with the case. The city is paralyzed, and Detective Lindsay Boxer is caught in the eye of the storm.

Will the Women's Murder Club make it out alive—or will a sudden courtroom snare ensure their last breaths?

SOME GAMES AREN'T FOR CHILDREN....

After a nasty divorce, Christy Moore finds her escape in Marty Hawking, who introduces her to all sorts of experiences, including an explosive new game called "Make-Believe."

But what begins as innocent fun soon turns dark, and as Marty pushes the boundaries farther and farther, the game just may end up deadly.

Read the new jaw-dropping thriller *Let's Play Make-Believe,* **available now from**

BOOK**SHOTS**

Looking to Fall in Love in Just One Night?
Introducing BookShots Flames:

original romances presented by James Patterson that fit into your busy life.

Featuring Love Stories by:

New York Times bestselling author Jen McLaughlin

New York Times bestselling author Samantha Towle

USA Today bestselling author Erin Knightley

Elizabeth Hayley

Jessica Linden

Codi Gary

Laurie Horowitz

…and many others!

Available only from

James Patterson's BOOKSHOTS Flames

HER SECOND CHANCE AT LOVE MIGHT BE TOO GOOD TO BE TRUE....

When Chelsea O'Kane escapes to her family's inn in Maine, all she's got are fresh bruises, a gun in her lap, and a desire to start anew. That's when she runs into her old flame, Jeremy Holland. As he helps her fix up the inn, they rediscover what they once loved about each other.

Until it seems too good to last…

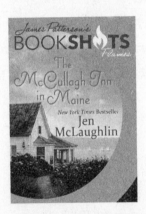

Read the stirring story of hope and redemption, *The McCullagh Inn in Maine*, available now from

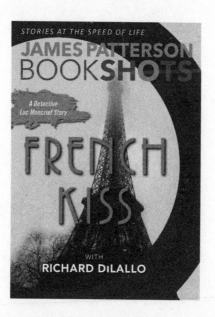